The Clay Queen

The Children of Clay, Volume 1

Ono Ekeh

Published by Ono Ekeh, 2017.

This is a work of fiction. Similarities to real people, places, or events are entirely coincidental.

THE CLAY QUEEN

First edition. October 22, 2017.

Copyright © 2017 Ono Ekeh.

Written by Ono Ekeh.

Dedication:

To my family

Legal:

All of the characters and events portrayed in this novel are either products of the author's imagination and/or are used fictitiously.

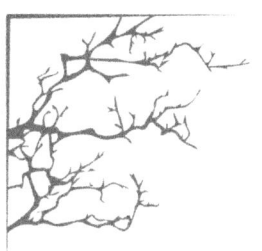

Prologue

THERE ARE TWO AND ONLY two gods, Ryna—pronounced *Rhee-nay*—the sky god and creator of all, and myself, Nouei, the earth god, the primordial clay. I am the fabled demiurge. I am eternal, indestructible, but not immutable. I have no powers of my own except what I receive from Ryna—but Ryna has no outlet for her powers except in me.

Ryna sees in me, a slave, and she, my benevolent mistress. I see in her my mother, and me, her child, though she recoils at the thought. "We are of different natures," she insists. She is being, and I am matter.

The Jaru mock me and my subjects because I do not fit their idea of a god. They say I am just like them: human, weak, fragile. *Why must it be said to be so? Why is it that you are not like me, gods?* Yes, I hunger and thirst, for I am human. I crave touch and warmth. I fear the dark, the pain, and the suffering. But how does that make me any less a god?

From where I sit, it is now four thousand years into the future from your present. The earth has been devastated by human hubris and, I shall confess, by my failure to broker peace. But that was two thousand years ago (from my present) and now, as my self-induced penance, I must bear in my bones the poison of the earth in order to preserve the very humans who mock me.

The Jaru, the Fenti, and others say I am a pathetic god. They laugh at the modesty of my temple. I like my temple. It is magnificent and befitting a god.

Even now, they march up north to demand that I kneel before the image of Ryna. They have every right to, because for the fifth time, by Ryna's aid, my people's military has been decimated and many of the

Low Country have abandoned me to worship Ryna. The Jaru march north, converting my people along the way. In a fortnight, they will arrive here at my temple gates.

Ryna controls time. It is in her power as the Almighty. I, on the other hand, am pure passivity. I am only what I am made to be. I take powers from whomever or whatever will offer them to me. I can absorb pain, fear, love, joy, hope, poison, anything—except evil. Evil is nothing and cannot exist.

I have set myself against Ryna for ages upon ages, and in each cycle, I am forced to return to my eternal state of passivity until she reanimates me. Except now.

After so many eons, I have finally absorbed the power of time.

There are two ways to see time. One, Ryna's way, is to perceive it as a linear progression toward the future. I cannot plan for the future, for I cannot see it. I see time the other way, the way it was not meant to be seen. I perceive time laterally, sprouting out of the present.

While Ryna marches forward, I march sideways.

And so now I write my story. Not the story of how I became a god, for I am and always will be one. But of how Ryna will recognize me as a god and must then receive me and love me as her child. My writings are hidden from Ryna. This is my prerogative. As long as I write my present and its possibilities, I write the future. If I finish telling my story, a story that spans from your present to three thousand years into my future, if I finish that story, a seven-thousand-year story, before the Jaru arrive at my temple in a fortnight, I will have won the race, for I will have changed the past before they get here. They will arrive to find me more powerful than they ever imagined.

Ryna animates me, but I animate potentiality.

I have three secrets.

I created the Selites, my pure children who preserve the pure passivity of the demiurge. Every time I am returned to my primordial state and Ryna begins again, they preserve the history of my existence, and I am thus no longer tabula rasa.

My second secret is that before my story is done, I will have created a new god. With her by my side, Ryna will no longer have the power to dispose of me as she wills. She must meet me as an equal.

I do not wish to speak ill of Ryna. There is no one I love more. Every dawn, my heart skips when I see her in the horizon, staring in wonder and fascination at the children of men. I have tried to emulate her in everything I have done. Everything but one. As desperate as I am for worship, I will not reap men's souls to satisfy my thirst. I strive to inspire all humanity to love me, and it is only when the intransigent are left that I will unleash my sword as he who will force the rest to bow before me.

I digress.

The Jaru march north.

I must begin my story if I am to rewrite seven thousand years of history before they arrive.

I begin with the marriage of two parallel worlds. One is a world of pure randomness—a zero-probability world. The other world is one of pure definitiveness, one-hundred-percent probability, where all that is probable... is.

This is my third secret. I have splintered the world out into all probable configurations. Ryna sees only absolutes. I see only probability. There is one absolute world—and a million probable worlds. Her world is somewhere on the spectrum of worlds. I don't know which one it is. I only know it is not world zero or world one hundred. I begin with these.

I am Nouei, and this is my opening gambit.

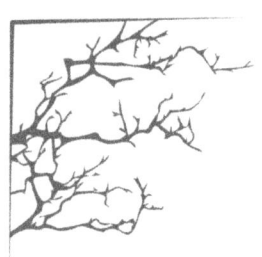

Chapter 1

"CONTAINMENT'S SECURE, Sir. Confirming energy transfer!" Captain Tumai called out.

A sharp crackling discharge rocked the room, causing everyone in the large, amphitheater-style control room to duck in fright. The lights flickered from the electrical surge but stabilized soon after.

"Prepare the Selites," Director Hera Tifo ordered. "Bring them in here, all two hundred." She inhaled as she watched the large containment area at the center of the room spark and fill up with a milky gas.

"We have to recreate the exact conditions, in case the Wave hits and we need to repeat this process," she said to Tumai.

"Yes, Sir." Tumai signaled toward the doors at the top tier of the room. A moment later, scores of Selites filed in and lined up against the back wall of the room's top tier. The Selites, Silicon-based creatures, humanoid at present, took on whatever form was required by their masters.

"Do we have the child?" Hera asked as she ran up toward the Selites. A man handed her a gurgling baby. "You're so delightful." Cooing at the child, she nuzzled its pudgy cheeks as she cradled it.

The Selites watched her expectantly as she inspected them. "On my authority, as a representative of the Council, you are to retain custody of this child, Theresa Bridget." She handed the baby carefully to one of them, who cradled the baby and rocked her gently. "We don't know if our energy bridge will hold successfully, but if—" she paused for emphasis— "if it holds and someone comes through, and if the Wave pulses, which means that everything will change, you are ordered to commit the child to the custody of our guest. Understood?"

4

"Understood." The Selite chorus echoed through the hall.

Hera leaned in and kissed a Selite who had reached out, and briefly hugged her. They were gluttons for affection, and she usually had that in spades to give them, but not now. There were other pressing matters at the moment.

The crackling in the containment chamber continued with loud bursts, drawing Hera's attention back down to the engineers—closer to the center of activity.

"Thank you," she whispered to the fragile-looking, dark crystalline beings who swayed gently, as though in an invisible wind.

They carefully passed the baby down the line and each one inspected her; some hugged her, others kissed her, while others rocked her.

Comforted at the sight, Hera made her way back down to the lower tiers. "Report."

"The density is sustainable. Particle distribution is… Sir! I think someone's coming through. These are not our quantum particles; these are new particles!" An excited voice responded from closer to the chamber. A ripple of excitement coursed through the hundreds of people in the room.

"The spins are locked in the same direction, and the field is in equilibrium," another voice yelled out. "There's perfect complementarity."

Tumai held Hera's shoulder. "Good God! A person. From index… one hundred?"

The room grew silent at the statement. Hera, like everyone, was stunned. In theory, it was true that such a world existed—a world of one-hundred percent probability distribution. It just wasn't comprehendible. A world so stable and ordered that its inhabitants naturally conceived no alternatives.

A loud boom sounded in the room, shaking all the fixtures, desks, and equipment. The lights flickered off, leaving the room in darkness. The backup generators started up, bringing the lights back on. Silence prevailed for a minute, followed by a flurry of activity as people rushed to the aid of those who'd fainted or were momentarily incapacitated.

"There's a person in there, Sir," a trembling Tumai said, pointing at a panel display, then peering into the smoky containment chamber.

Hera rushed toward the containment and hesitated at the door. Her heart thumped loudly in her ears and her hands trembled. She'd wet herself from the boom earlier, but nothing was going to stop her from seeing this project through.

The door whirled open and a vacuum sucked the gases from the containment chamber. Writhing on the ground was a naked woman, moaning in agony. Hera turned to the Selite next to her. "Observe. If the Wave occurs, continue our prescribed course of action."

Hera rushed to the shaking woman and knelt in front of her. "You're safe, sweetheart. You're safe."

The woman was apparently in the throes of a seizure, foaming at the mouth as her milky eyeballs rolled back and forth.

"Four-hundred milligrams phenobarbitone," Hera called out as others joined her in the chamber.

"No, wait," a woman said as she listened to the heart. "Her heartbeat's over two hundred a minute."

Hera took a deep breath. "Continue the seizure medication. Apply ice to her eyes and compress the carotid bulb; let's see if that slows the heart rate."

They watched the woman's vitals on a monitor as they cleaned her and wrapped warmed blankets around her.

"Seizure's better, but heartrate's climbing."

A voice filled the chamber. "The Academy just sent a Wave advisory. Fifteen minutes."

"What's the Order's estimate?" Tumai asked.

"Six minutes."

Tumai looked at Hera, who gave a slight nod.

"Go with the Order's estimate," she said. Still kneeling, she leaned back on her heels and watched their guest, holding her hand. Such courage to have undertaken an uncertain journey between worlds. The chances of success were incredibly low. But it made sense that someone from index one hundred would have the ultimate faith in her abilities. How strange a world it must be to never doubt yourself because there was never an alternative to consider.

"Hera, the heartrate's still over two hundred. It's slowed a little, but if the Order is right, we don't have time."

"Very well. Twelve milligrams of adenosine," she responded. "Prep the defibrillator, get the electrodes ready."

Tumai looked up at the time clock. "Hera. Restart the heart. There's no time."

"Her body has been through so much..."

"I know," he said softly. "But the heartrate's regular. She seems strong—"

"Okay, stay the adenosine. Twenty milligrams, calcium channel blocker," Hera said.

"Blood pressure's seventy over forty!"

Hera stroked the guest's short curly hair. "I'm sorry," she whispered. Looking up to her team. "Continue the blocker. At thirty seconds to the Wave threshold, apply the electrodes!"

Tumai looked at the Selites. "When the Wave pulses, take over!"

"Heartrate's still too high."

"Applying electrodes, defibrillator is charged and ready!"

"Thirty seconds to Wave," Tumai called out.

"Selites, move in," Hera ordered. "Everyone clear!" She pushed the button and the woman's body pumped off the ground and landed back with a thud.

"I feel it." A man to Hera's right smiled and inhaled. "The Order's estimate was correct."

"I love you all so much. I'll see you beyond the Wave. May Ryna bless us all," Hera said as she lay flat on the ground. She never heard the responses. The Wave pulsed.

VESTA GROANED AS SHE opened her eyes. She sat up and looked around at dozens of quiet eyes staring at her. The moderately-sized room was filled to capacity. The bed under her was soft, but it made a loud squeak whenever she moved.

A man knelt next to her. "Greetings. I am Director Tumai." Pointing to a woman who'd crouched next to him, "She's Captain Hera Tifo." He took Vesta's hand.

"Where am I?" Vesta asked.

"You are where you are supposed to be," Hera said. "Does that make sense to you?" Hera pressed a soft patch with a sticky gel onto Vesta's neck. "This will calm you and help you relax."

Vesta leaned back on the wall behind her and closed her eyes. Strong arms enveloped her and laid her back on the bed.

"I bring greetings from... I bring... I greet you..."

Soft lips kissed her forehead. "Go to sleep and rest. We will be here when you awake. You are safe."

Shuffling sounds filled the room, and then all was silent.

Vesta woke again to the sounds of excited whispers. The room was the same, although the walls were a colorful and odd mix of brick and concrete, unlike what she thought she remembered. Again, the room was filled to capacity.

"I'm sorry," Vesta whispered, her mouth dry. She sat up slowly. "I meant to be more prepared. We trained—"

Unable to suppress a wave of nausea, she vomited on a woman who had been kneeling next to the bed. The woman made no attempt to move or even react in disgust.

"You will feel better soon. My name is Captain Hera Tifo, and this is Director Tumai to my right."

Vesta leaned her elbows on her knees and closed her eyes to orient herself. She opened them to see Hera being cleaned. She'd taken her shirt and underclothes off, and a shiny, grayish being helped wipe her and put on a new shirt.

"What is that?" Vesta pointed at the metallic gray creature.

"They are Selites. Silicon-based lifeforms," Tumai said. "Welcome to the world of all alternatives, the world of zero probability distribution. You made it." His rich baritone words rushed into each other as though he were so excited to speak the next word that he could not wait to articulate the current one.

Hera sat next to Vesta. "Do you have the Wave in your world?"

"I don't know what that is," Vesta replied. The dozens of spectators kept their eyes locked on her. She felt like a specimen, as she discerned pure wonder in their gazes.

"There is no continuity here. When the Wave pulses at random intervals, everything changes," Tumai said. "The Selites, though, can preserve information from Wave to Wave. We depend on them to preserve knowledge. They are our slaves."

"They don't change with your Wave?" Vesta asked.

Tumai shrugged. "We think they succumb eventually. The change is delayed with them. We don't know why."

"Here." Hera offered Vesta a bowl of green fruit. "Replenish your strength. We don't have much time. The Wave may pulse again in three hours, according to our estimates. You've been asleep for twenty hours."

"But you said the Wave was random?"

"Yes," Hera said, looking momentarily confused. "Randomness means it fits no existing pattern or algorithm, but it doesn't mean we are without a sense of the Wave's advent. There are those among us who are attuned to the Wave, and they register their perceptions with the Academy and with the Order."

Vesta closed her eyes and felt Hera's strong hands help her down to the pillow. Her mouth still felt dry, but the fruit had helped. Her chest was sore, as was her throat. In her head was a distant thud, like the remnant of a very bad headache. She opened her eyes, grateful for the room's soft and warm tones. The walls were a muted lime-green color, with waves of various greens streaming across. Along the walls were hundreds of small square plaques with writing on them.

"What are those squares?" she asked.

Tumai leaned over her, filling her vision. "We tried hard to think of what things we do that would appear strange to you. But this didn't occur to us. I'm glad you asked. They are labels and instructions for when things change."

"They look like symbols," Vesta said. "Is this your writing?"

"Between Wave pulses, the alphabet, grammar, and mathematics of the next wave are perceptible. As the Wave approaches, these squares translate our labels and instructions, so wherever we end up, we have some orientation for what to do. For instance, if you became ill. I don't know what skills I have, but I know there are instructions around here to help me. After a Wave, I may appear next to a piece of equipment; the labels will tell me what it is and how to operate it."

"Wow. This is bizarre," Vesta said. "I wish my people could see this, could be here." She sat up again, this time feeling more stable. "Is there a duplicate version of me in this world?"

"Yes," Tumai said. "But we wouldn't know where or how to find her. If she's meant to be here, she will be."

"Why are they all staring at me?" Vesta asked, nodding her head toward the silent crowd who'd watched the entire interaction.

The room broke into gentle murmurs and giggles as the people turned away and talked to each other quietly.

"Is this not the way of your people?" Hera asked, her lips teasing a smile at the edges.

Vesta shook her head as she chewed hungrily at another fruit.

"I apologize. You understand, don't you... to see someone from a parallel world. It's a wonder," Tumai said. "May I ask... what God you worship?"

"Her name is Thysia," Vesta replied.

The people gasped and stared in silence.

"We follow the Most High, the One than whom nothing greater can be conceived," Vesta said. "Surely you must worship her, too? How else could we have found each other?"

Hera smiled. "Our God is Ryna—pronounced, rhee-nay. The subject and term, the object of all love. She is love itself."

Vesta took in a deep breath and edged to the tip of the bed. "Our Thysia, she is the one before whom all words—"

"Recoil?" Hera completed with a smile. "The one before whom all words recoil? Your Thysia is our Ryna!"

The room erupted in muted cheers. Vesta watched in amusement as they shook hands and congratulated each other.

"Does the word 'believe' mean anything to you?" Tumai asked.

"In a speculative sense, yes," Vesta replied. "But no one actually believes. You either know or you don't."

Hera's eyes opened in clear fascination. "Know? What is that?"

"It must be our correlate," Vesta said. "You, in this world, believe. In ours, we know."

Tumai whispered to Hera, "I think 'know' is faith in immutable order." He shook his head as though incredulous. "We found them. We actually found them. She is from index one hundred."

"I'm glad I'm here," Vesta said. "I must confess, it's less haphazard that I expected."

"You confuse random for chaos," Hera said. "The random is generated by being, while chaos is the absence of being. Chaos has no hope of order even with the intervention of being."

Vesta chuckled. "We spent hours theorizing about randomness. There is no difference for us between randomness and chaos. But it is a distinction that is clear to you."

"Our world is simply a non-recurring permutation of an infinite set of things," Hera said with a smile. "Purple is still purple. I am me... essences, though fluid, remain. It's the combinations that change."

Vesta closed her eyes as she tried to follow Hera's line of thought.

Tumai continued. "Randomness is a pure expression of the beauty of being, just as absolute order, on the other end of the spectrum, is the expression of beauty. Since not everything is God, but everything that is not God is created, then that which is not God is inherently random prior to its formal configuration. Our world is that instance of creation on the edge of form. We are the instant divine ideas become real."

"In ours, everything is nature," Vesta said. "One never deviates from what one is."

"We've done much talking," Tumai said. "Would you like to rest?"

"No, thank you. There's a reason I'm here, and we must attend to that."

"Our world is collapsing," Hera said, holding Vesta's hands.

"As is ours," Vesta responded. "We figured that if we were collapsing, so would the complement world. It was why we created the bridge to find you. If both our worlds fail, it'll trigger a cascading failure in all parallel worlds between us on the probability distribution spectrum."

Tumai took a deep breath and signaled to a Selite. "We can't leave this building, but we have been authorized by our World Council to act on behalf of the people. Our world is one of absolute discontinuity. This building shields us from the Wave for a time, after which we succumb to it, as does everyone else out there. We need you to understand that as we speak or interact, everything may change. If Wave pulses this moment, you'll find yourself dealing with another person, another Director. The Selites will preserve any information and ensure continuity for you. That is, if you remain unaffected."

"With our shielding, the variations in this building are limited," Hera said. "You'll still find yourself dealing with one of us here until the Wave reclaims all. Hopefully, you'll be gone by then."

Vesta stood on unsteady legs. "How can you live this way? With this inherent randomness?"

"I know it is strange to you, but the order and rigidness of anything else is terrifying," Hera said. "We live in complete joy of the spontaneity of our lives. To do otherwise would mean to be burdened with the future and oppressed by order."

"Can you plan for the future?" Vesta asked.

"No, but, why would you?" Tumai asked. "We think there was a time in our distant evolution when some of us could, but nature selected them out. This is no world for planners, only for those who live in the moment."

"Do you wake up in the morning to a different woman or man in your bed? A different wife or husband?"

Hera smiled at Vesta's clear incredulity. "We own no one. We are all wives and husbands, girlfriends and boyfriends, fathers, mothers, sons, and daughters. Yes, we wake up to discontinuity, and love whoever is there before us. You, now, are here before me. And I love you with all my heart."

"Such freedom," Vesta marveled. "So pure. So naïve. Would you all like to get chairs and sit? I am in awe of you, as you must be of me, and I love having you all here."

Excited chatter filled the room, all eyes still focused on Vesta, who was still standing as everyone sat on the floor around her.

Vesta laughed in delight at the childlike behavior.

A young man walked up to her, clothes in his hand. He began to remove Vesta's shirt. Vesta stepped back in surprise, almost tipping over. "No, thank you. I can manage if you'll just give me those."

He looked confused. "I thought the gold would match your skin tone, and the scarf, your eyes. They are a beautiful blend of gray and green."

She smiled. "That is so sweet of you. But I'm fine with what I have on. It'll do." She looked around and all eyes were on her. "Oh, dear. Did I say something wrong?"

Tumai held her hand. "You have not wronged us. But why…"

"Consent," Vesta whispered to herself. "You have no concept of consent, do you?"

"Consent?" Tumai said. "The expression of gratitude?"

"No," Vesta laughed. "I mean to agree to a choice. This young man offered me those clothes, but I gave no consent for him to dress me."

"You mean you might not want him to dress you?" Hera gasped. She looked at Tumai. "I suppose that makes sense."

"You just dress each other when you feel like it?" Vesta asked.

"Yes," Hera said. "If I have something that will be a good fit for you, I give it to you and you receive it. My regrets. We worked so hard to understand what you might be like, but I fear we failed."

"No. You have been most wonderful hosts. I will receive the clothes. You may dress me."

The man approached tentatively, but Vesta beamed at him. He was joined by others who removed her clothes, washed her, and clothed her, while others worked on her hair. She was itching to talk about the world collapse problem, but they seemed to have no concern for time.

It had been thirty minutes, and Vesta desperately wanted to look in a mirror to see what they'd done to her. She was unsure about the etiquette of such a request, though. She guessed one simply accepted a gift and did not second-guess its quality. The shoes, made of a tightly woven straw-like fabric, looked like they'd be prickly, but were rather comfortable. Her underclothes had been replaced by a singular tight outfit that covered from her ankles to her shoulders, and out to her wrists. Like the shoes, it was far more comfortable than it looked. A gold button-down dress with elbow-length sleeves and a wide waistband completed the outfit. She couldn't see her hair, but from all the looks she got, they were impressed. She felt elegant, even if such a feeling was out of place at this time.

"Is this a good time to talk more about why I am here?" Vesta asked.

"Absolutely," Tumai said. "We would love to hear your thoughts. We could use your guidance."

"Based on our analysis," Vesta said, "the collapse of our two worlds is intentional—someone has set out to destroy us—all of us. I realize this may not be clear to you. When we figured that our world was headed to destruction, as was yours, we made plans for contact. In the process, we did an analysis of what we thought you would be like. It occurred to us that you may not understand the concept of violence."

Everyone looked back and forth at each other. A voice, tentative, spoke up. "Do you mean, to cause harm?"

"Yes, precisely that," Vesta replied. "But to do so intentionally."

Her statement was greeted by a collective horrified gasp. There was commotion as the Selites were whisked from the room and several others departed, leaving Vesta with Tumai, Hera, and a handful of people.

"Did I say something wrong?" Vesta asked.

"No," Hera said, holding Vesta's hand. She massaged Vesta's fingers gently. "We believe theoretically that there is a concept of evil—we just don't know it, and most importantly, we must never imprint that idea on the Selites. This is why they were removed."

"Why?"

"They are pure passivity," Hera said. "They have no personalities or independence, as far as we can tell. All they are, all they have, is what we give to them. They are elements of pure love because it is all we have, though in various degrees. But if they were exposed to evil, then such evil would persist in them for eternity. If the Selites are corrupted, they would introduce that evil into our world. It would change us and affect the entire spectrum of worlds by consequence. Our world anchors love and goodness in the human spectrum of worlds. The Selites anchor *us* in our goodness and love. Their purity is an utmost priority for us."

"How did they come to be? Did you make them? Or did they evolve?"

"We don't know. They've always been with us," Tumai said. "They tell us they are a gift from the gods."

"Gods?" Vesta asked in surprise.

"Yes. I see your confusion," Tumai said. "We, too, don't understand what they mean. There is only one God, Ryna. But it is what they say, and we trust them."

He took Vesta by the hand. "We are glad you're here. We can't leave our world. We would never survive in any other world, but *you* can survive in every world. But our gifts, our faith, our perception of all things probable are perhaps what will save us all. Come with me. Let us show you how you can help." He led her back into the large adjoining amphitheater, at the center of which was the containment chamber.

"A baby?" Vesta asked, hearing soft cries.

"Yes," Hera said. "The Selites tell us that since she was born, she counters the Wave sometimes. She appears to have the capacity to anticipate and preserve a measure of sameness. She's us—but so much more."

A Selite laid the cooing baby in Hera's arms, and Hera in turn gave her to Vesta.

"She's beautiful," Vesta whispered. "How old is she?"

"We don't know. Age is not relevant to us."

Vesta turned to the Selite to offer her thanks, but Hera stood in front of her, her neck muscles taut and her face twitching. "You must never speak to them. You are a violent woman. I mean no disrespect."

"Why can't I speak to them?" Vesta asked, confused. "You have no violence in your world at all?"

Hera shook her head. "We only know love. No one has ever committed—or will ever intentionally commit—harm in our world. Yes, violence and evil are logical possibilities when you think of them in contrast to good, but goodness that has evil as a contrast is an impoverished idea of the good."

Vesta countered, "We assume that every parallel world on the spectrum has evil. But maybe yours, as a zero-probability world, is the only one that doesn't."

"Yes. And no other world has the Selites. We must not risk having you contaminate them by speaking to them," Hera said. "I will thank it for you."

"Sure. I apologize," Vesta said. "I meant no offense." The eyes around her bore no malice, and seemed befuddled by her apology.

"She may be able to save us," Tumai said, pointing to the child in Vesta's arms.

"We have enough power to generate another bridge, hopefully before the next Wave. We will send her with you to any world, and maybe she can help save us," Hera said.

"We have determined the optimal world in which to operate," Vesta said. "It is perfectly balanced, and I have the perfect situation in mind, if you can get me there." She took special notice when Tumai and Hera looked at each other.

"What's wrong now?" she said, worried that she'd said or done something wrong.

"We must send some Selites with you, so that the baby always has memories and all their gifts at her disposal. The Selites will enter her and live in her body."

"Ah! The challenge," Vesta said. "In whatever world I choose, the Selites must be preserved from the stain of evil."

Her hosts nodded. "No one must ever know. The power and possibilities they offer is much too great for anyone not of our world."

"So if the Selites must live in this child, she must then be preserved from the stain of evil so as not to sully them?"

She received nods of agreement.

"But how?" Vesta looked back and forth. "That would be impossible, especially in the world I will take her to."

"She must be raised like us," Tumai said. "She must not follow your Thysia, but Ryna, wholeheartedly. It is only then that she will be preserved from evil and will not stain the Selites. Your Thysia permits evil. Ryna does not."

"It means that you must not raise her or have contact with her," Hera said. "Your world is a violent one. We've imagined that you would have no hesitation to use violence if it were justified in your eyes."

"This is true," Vesta said. "For us, things are or are not. I suppose when you believe you know truth, any disagreement is the first step to conflict. We are very combative, but we do eventually resolve all issues with truth."

They all stared at her. The entire amphitheater was silent.

"I give you my word. I will not raise her, nor contact her. She will be raised with knowledge of Ryna alone." She exhaled as she witnessed the apprehension melting from the faces of her hosts.

"I have one request, though, before we leave," Vesta said.

"Absolutely," Hera said. "Everything we have is for everyone else. Any request will be granted."

"Can you ask one of the Selites who this baby is and what is her story? Her history?"

"History?"

"Yes. What things have happened to her?"

Tumai took a deep breath. "We don't have such a concept, but I will ask." He turned to a Selite. "Tell us about the events of this child. All its previous present moments."

In a moment of commotion, all the Selites rushed to gather together. They lined up in the aisle going upward, and in unison began to recite the history of the child Theresa Bridget.

"The chronicles of Theresa Bridget, the re-incarnation of Nouei, god and Queen of the Ashwan." Their majestic voices paused in precise unity and then started up again. "The words of Queen Siyesu, god of the Puthna. Mother of the Selites. There is nothing like being married to a God. There is nothing like being loved by a God. There is nothing so vibrant..."

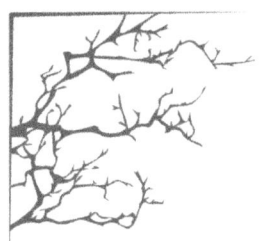

Chapter 2

THE TWO RYNEAN SISTERS, one standing, the other kneeling, steadied themselves against the wind circling the cavern shaft. Another gust sent the ritual book of prayers flying out of Sister Vesta Kaypore's hands, sending it deep into the darkness of the cavern. It didn't matter. All that mattered was for Sister Qhy to maintain her resolve.

Sister Kaypore secured her green scarf to her robe. "Is this your testimony, Sister Qhy?" she asked.

The fawn-like woman met her gaze. "I saw the blue light of Ryna. In this very cavern. This is my testimony."

Sister Kaypore tried to recall the next step of the death ritual. Sister Qhy had to consent to die. "Is this your will? To die to preserve our secret, our Order?"

The young woman held both of Sister Kaypore's hands between her smooth palms. "The path to the land of my Fathers has been opened for me; illuminated by the light of Ryna. If it please the Lord, dismiss me and let me go—into Lord Rynae's bosom."

Sister Kaypore regarded the young Sister. She had only been with the Order of Ryna for five months, but now she was to be taken from them—the fate of all who see the light. She wanted to crouch and hug her, but she had to be steadfast. If she couldn't encourage the ritual to completion, she couldn't demand steadfastness of anyone else; most of all, the young woman kneeling before her.

"Please don't cry." Sister Qhy stood and reached out to comfort the stately elder Sister. "I am frightened... and happy." She wiped Sister Kaypore's tears with her hands and peered downward, deep into the darkness. No one knew what was down there. Sister Kaypore's muffled cries continued as Sister Qhy stood by the glass wall that separated the cavern shaft from the great hall behind her called "The Cavern Room."

All the Order's resident Brothers and Sisters at the Monastery of Light had come to see her off. Behind the glass wall, hundreds of their silent, intent faces, betraying no grief, willed her on. Euthanasia, they called it. The sweet death. The death of one's choosing. The purest sacrifice for Ryna.

She touched the glass wall. A hand on the other side touched the glass, too. She blew a soft kiss and sniffled as she saw their faces melt into tears. Taking a deep breath, she turned and approached the short railing at the cavern's edge. Sister Kaypore reached out with a copper vessel full of earth. She scooped out a generous amount and poured it into Sister Qhy's hands.

The young Sister's tears fell on the soil as she balled it tight and cradled it. "To dust," she whispered to herself.

Sister Kaypore, in halting breaths that faded with each word, intoned the departing prayer. "The golden cord is broken. The flower of the earth is returned to thee." Wiping her tear-stained face, she opened a latch, revealing an opening in the railing at the threshold of the cavern shaft.

Sister Qhy, holding the earth in her hand, looked at the last living person she would see. She swallowed. "I would have loved to see the Miracle of the Sun."

"I wish you could have," Sister Kaypore replied. "It's beautiful."

"My mother saw it—the flaming orb kisses the rainbow. She said that you can look directly at the sun as it dances in the sky; it bobbles and twists and shoots down toward us." She turned back to the cavern. "It's one reason I joined the Order."

"I'm so sorry," Sister Kaypore replied.

"Don't be. I am going to the real Sun and her Angel, beyond the shadows of this world." She paused. "In two weeks, when you watch the sun, will you remember me?"

"I will," Sister Kaypore replied. "And when you come into the presence of Ryna, in the land without shadow, remember us." Her face twitched. "I love you so much." *Don't hug her. Don't touch her. Let her go.*

"I love you too, Sister," Sister Qhy's whisper, through quivering lips, cut through the howling gusts. Sister Kaypore nodded, allowing her tears to flow freely now.

Sister Qhy stood at the edge of the cavern and crossed her forearms over her chest. She took another deep breath. "Nunc dimittis." She closed her eyes and let herself drop deep into the darkness.

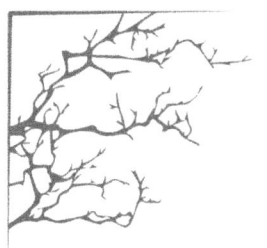

Chapter 3

JEREMY BLADE SPLASHED water on his face and looked into the mirror. He straightened his blue shirt, buttoned his cuffs, and smiled at his reflection. Not bad for having slept on park benches for the last four nights. *Bridget*, he thought with a sigh. He needed to get back to Bridget, his wife, whom he'd left outside the South American snake exhibit. It was never a good idea to leave her unsupervised for long.

"Long day?"

Jeremy turned to a large middle-aged man washing his hands. He chuckled. "Honeymoon. Five years late."

"Congratulations," the man said, wiping his hands. "Couldn't have picked a better spot than Paris. American?"

Jeremy nodded and reached out his hand. "Jeremy Blade."

"Jeremy Blade? I know you." The man's eyes widened. "You're the special science economy guy the president appointed—"

"To lead the Economic and Technological Innovation Council. Yes."

"Well, Dr. Blade, you're looking at a live, walking, talking product of all your good work. You're a good man, and just as handsome in person. You should've seen my wife every time you showed up on the news. My Lord. She would be absolutely hysterical. She has all your books: *The Market Quotient, Quantifying your Brand*, and she's reading the one on leadership."

Jeremy's eyes narrowed. "I have more books—"

"I know it's not all of them," the man chuckled. "There're all those complicated finance things you write, but she figured the other books put your ideas into layman's terms. She wants me to read them. Hey!

Maybe I can develop and sell a company for a cool few hundred million. Didn't you just do that a few months ago? Any stray ideas lying around?"

Jeremy smiled. "You'll be the first to know. I'm sorry, I have to check on my wife. It was a pleasure meeting you."

Jeremy rushed out of the bathroom into the dark corridor and toward the exhibit. He oriented himself as he looked both ways. The large paneled exhibits on either side were all clear, in contrast to all the activity a few minutes ago. Odd. No one was interested in any other reptile exhibit except the South American snake exhibit, down the corridor where he'd left Bridget. Hurrying to the exhibit, he pressed through the thick crowd, calling for his wife.

Jeremy, taller than the average person, scanned over the heads of the crowd. "Bridget!" he yelled.

Turning at the collective gasp, his heart skipped a beat at the sight of Bridget—in the enclosure! She was on her haunches; her hand was stretched over a small pool of water, reaching toward a snake wound tightly over a piece of wood. Her lips were moving. She was talking to something.

"Bridget! No. No. No."

Panicked, he forced his way through the crowd and ran his hands along the wall until he found a door to the right of the enclosure. He tugged it open, revealing a confined, dark hallway with back entrances into the reptile enclosures. He locked the door behind him.

"Madame! Madame! No!"

Jeremy ran toward the voice.

"Sir, you cannot be here." A uniformed man waved him away.

"*C'est mon épouse*—That's my wife," Jeremy said, in fluent French. He pressed his face against the door. "Bridget!"

The snake reached toward her—its pale green skin, which was dotted with yellow spots, shimmered in the enclosure's light. Its underbelly and the bottom half of its head were a deep mustard yellow. Its forked tongue flicked as it recoiled. Its strike was much faster than Jeremy thought possible. Bridget, crouched in front of the snake, fell backward and grimaced.

"Bridget!" Jeremy screamed. He tugged on the door and pounded on the glass. "*Ouvrez la porte*—Open the door!"

"Excuse me, sir." The man pushed Jeremy aside and rushed into the exhibit with a long metal pole, tapered at the end with a large hook. He took slow, careful steps. "Madame, you must come with me. You've been bitten."

Bridget, her face contorted in obvious pain, followed him slowly, mimicking his careful steps until they exited the enclosure.

"Sweetheart," she said, her voice full of obvious relief. "You're here."

"What were you thinking?" Jeremy yelled. He lifted her t-shirt and crouched to inspect the bite on her torso.

"We must get an antidote." The curator, agitated, dropped his rod. "We have little time. That was our most venomous snake. I don't know why I let you in there."

Jeremy stopped the man. "No. Just give us a second here. Please."

The man stared at Jeremy with knotted eyebrows. "Sir?"

Bridget winced at Jeremy's touch.

"Are you okay?" Jeremy asked her, quietly. "Tell me what to do."

"I'll be fine," she said, with eyes closed and fists clenched. "Let's go. There's still a few places we have to visit this evening." She remained still, as though afraid to move.

"Will your body take care of the venom?" Jeremy asked in a whisper.

She nodded and smiled at him. Her face relaxed, returning to its natural spectral beauty. She always looked and moved as though she were a ghost trapped in this world. "Let's go."

"But Madame, you must get treatment," the curator said.

"Should we at least get some of the venom? Jeremy asked.

"Can you and Bede synthesize it?" she asked.

"Yes. It can't be that hard." Jeremy leaned into her ear. "Make him give you the snake."

She smirked and whispered back, "You're just being naughty now. We don't need the whole snake—just a vial of venom."

"Yes, but we haven't done this before," Jeremy said. "It'll take a few tries. Look, the only other option is to take you to a hospital—"

She shook her head. "Okay," she said with a sigh.

She moved Jeremy to the side and addressed the curator in perfect French. "Sir, I know you are worried, but you need not be. Nothing in nature will kill me. I don't die. I suffer. I suffer greatly, but that's all. This pain will pass with time." She touched his shoulder lightly and looked into his face. "An antidote will not be the difference between me living or dying, but it may reduce my pain. I feel pain much more than anyone. It is amplified in my body and doesn't stop until it's run its course. If you let me take the snake, my husband and his brother can synthesize an antidote. I would be very grateful and I will never forget you."

The man stood, unmoving, as though waiting for her to say more. He then snapped out of his trance and nodded. Picking up the rod, he re-entered the enclosure, and returned a minute later with the snake twined around his snake pole. He motioned them to his workspace further down, and once there, forced the snake into a sack and then gently into a plastic container with a handle.

"Thank you, sir," Jeremy said, picking up the container. He handed the man his business card. "I don't know how you'll explain all this. God knows, I can't. Contact my office, we'll make sure you're taken care of."

Bridget pulled Jeremy out through the door, past confused employees who'd been trying to get in. They disappeared through the crowds and ran until they had left the zoo.

THE CLAY QUEEN

BRIDGET, CROSSED-LEGGED on a bench, watched in amusement as Jeremy wolfed down his third dinner of the evening—this one from the roadside stand across the brightly-lit square.

He mopped up the sauce from his roasted lamb stew with what was left of his flatbread. "This is delicious."

"You've said that five times now," she laughed. "I believe you. We ate at *Le Quatrieme* and *Le Palais*, two of the world's finest restaurants, tonight, and you hardly said anything about the quality of the food there."

He stopped eating his meal and looked up at her. "I said something about the wines." He cocked his head in the direction of his backpack.

She rolled her eyes. "You've been surly and bad-tempered all through the attractions and sights. The only times you've been happy, besides now, have been when I became your little experiment. You light up then. It makes you so happy."

"Aren't you ever curious about just how far this can go?" He wiped his mouth with a napkin. "At each restaurant, we ordered up to a thousand dollars worth of food, including these very expensive bottles of a rather fine vintage. All free. Thanks to you and those eyes of yours."

"It's not my eyes." Shuddering at the mention of her eyes, which she thought were large, set too deep, and cold—discolored whites like soured cream framing her uniformly night-black pupils and irises.

"Well, whatever spell you cast, it works," he laughed. "We could rule the world."

"It's not a spell," she said. "They do it willingly and I resent your taking advantage of it."

"I didn't force you."

"But you know I can't say no to you," she said.

"Someday, I will put our Rynean vows to the test. I will ask you to give me the world." He swung his arms wide in a grand gesture.

"Remember that our marriage vows work both ways," she said. "I can demand of you as much as you can demand of me."

"I'm not worried. I've always said I would give you anything I have to give."

Her heart swelled at his declaration. There was never any hesitation from him. All that he was and will be was hers. He was always so sure, so trusting of her, so willing to put his life in her hands.

"The world is not mine to give," she said.

"But it could be, with a million more spells like today."

"You act like it's the first time you've seen me do it."

"It's always the first time. I can never get used to it," he said.

"It's not a spell. All I do is get them to see me, and—"

"They fall in love with you. Yes, I know," he chuckled. "It is impossible to not fall in love with you. If any other Rynean heard you say this, it would be blasphemy. Eros is Ryna's alone. She alone is irresistible. You're flirting with heresy."

"I love Ryna more than anyone alive. I'm just speaking the truth as I know it."

"Someday, we'll meet someone who is impervious to you," he said.

"That could mean only one thing—that he or she already knows and loves me and cannot be induced to love me more."

"So if we met a man who—"

"Jeremy," she said, cutting him off. "It's our honeymoon. There'll never be another. For someone who has so much and is so steadfast, you're really insecure when it comes to me. I've made a vow to you. I will give you the world if I ever have it to give."

"You'll never have it to give." He sat back and looked at her. His mood had morphed from light playfulness to barely perceptible disdain. "You can make individuals or small groups love you. But love is limited. Fear is much more effective. What you accomplish in weeks with love, I can do in hours with fear. I can call up the President of the United States right now and he'd take my call."

"And yet," she countered triumphantly, "here you are with me, sleeping on park benches because I ask you to. This is why I love you.

You are my slave. Yes, you may coerce and dominate the world, but you will lay it at my feet because you love me."

Jeremy folded his arms and looked out toward the busy square.

"Can we not talk about this right now? I just want us to have a nice time tonight," she said.

After a minute had passed—"I saw you check on the snake," Jeremy said. "Snake all right?"

"A little lethargic, but I got to feed it right after it bit me. It's nourished."

"You got to feed it," he repeated. "You say that like it's nothing. Does it ever occur to you what you put us through with your crazy escapades?"

"Jeremy, not this again. You said you weren't angry."

"Well, I lied," he said. "Last year it was wild mushrooms. They didn't even look safe and you ate them. And almost died. I sat there day after day after day. Do you understand what Bede and I went through? What we go through worrying about what crazy thing you're going to do next?"

"Jeremy, I'm sorry. It wasn't supposed to turn out that way."

"Oh, really?" he said. "How exactly was it meant to turn out? You enter into a venomous snake habitat, reach out for the snake, and you expect *what*, exactly?"

She swallowed and turned away from him. She hated it when he was angry, but it was worse when his anger at her was not undeserved. She'd done so well these past four days just to make this honeymoon a memorable experience, and in one impulsive action, she'd tainted the whole experience.

Ten minutes later, breaking the silence that had persisted between them, he asked softly, "What are you thinking?"

"Calculating probabilities. See our buddy there?" She pointed at the food stand where Jeremy had bought one of tonight's dinners. "I thought I'd predict his customer rate in the next ten minutes and compare it to the sandwich guy." She smiled at him. "I thought I'd use a discrete probability distribution, like Poisson's."

"An exponential calculation in your head? Now you're just showing off."

She squeezed his hand in response.

"I suppose this is what happens when a theoretician and a mathematician go on their honeymoon," Jeremy said.

"We could do this together?"

"Is this where we're sleeping tonight?"

"Yes," she said.

"Sure. Let's start again. I'll get the average on my lamb-stew guy and you get the sandwich man."

She snuggled up to him and leaned on his shoulder.

"How are you feeling?" he asked.

"I'm fine."

Both knew she wasn't. She was in excruciating pain from the venom, but all they could do was wait and hope her body expelled it soon.

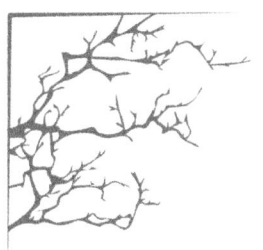

Chapter 4

"WE'RE LATE!" JEREMY called out in a huff, pulling his head back into the slowing taxi. He fumbled to unlatch his seat belt. "Paris could've waited," he grumbled. "Pull up here; *ici, Monsieur*! *Merci*!"

He cast a disapproving look at Bridget, who was already unbuckled and halfway out of the car before it rolled to a complete stop. He thrust a wad of bills into the eager hands of the taxi driver. Bridget had hauled their bags out of the trunk and deposited them on the sidewalk.

Jeremy hit the car's trunk to signal that they were clear and watched it weave dangerously among the crush of excited, chattery pilgrims wandering across the road that cut across the sprawling monastery grounds.

Bridget rubbed his back. "Don't worry, no one's going to get hurt. Ryna always protects her pilgrims. It's a documented fact. No one's ever been hurt at the Miracle of the Sun."

Ignoring her, Jeremy peered into the sky, waiting for a cloud to pass and reveal the sun.

Bridget scanned the vibrant crowd. "We haven't missed anything. Look around. No one's kneeling yet."

"You're right." He rubbed his jawline, fingering the five-day stubble growth, and patted his hair with both hands. "But you didn't know that. We could have missed it," he snapped.

Thousands of festive pilgrims, young and old, danced to the beat of dozens of wandering drummers who sought willing dancers. Horn and string musicians gathered in groups, blaring their improvised melodies. Pilgrims whirled together to the rhythms, creating a colorful fluorescent spectacle. Solitary dancers were not uncommon, but they were quickly joined by others who clapped the rhythm or joined in the dance. Scores of pilgrims, walking around with bags of bread bowls slung over their shoulders, were followed by those with pots of stew, thickening the air with the rich aroma of spices. Vendors hawked their religious artifacts and shirts, many with *I saw the Miracle of the Sun* written across the front.

Bridget beamed and slid her backpack over her shoulders, tightening the clasps around her muscular frame. She hopped onto one of the dozen stone benches lining the sidewalk and stood on tiptoe to catch a glimpse of the Monastery of Light in the distance, its gray façade and large columns set against the massive rock face into which it was carved. The dense crowds and the trees throughout the expansive grounds obstructed her view. All she could see clearly was one of the few approved images of the Blessed Almighty, Ryna, and her angel, a giant statue set atop the monastery—imposing, even from this distance.

"It's... a mile," she said, turning to Jeremy with a broad smile and eyes bright with anticipation.

He removed his jacket, stuffed it into his bag, and slung on his backpack. "Bede is probably losing his mind. We shouldn't have taken the Paris trip."

She stepped down from the stone bench. "It was not a trip, Sweetheart. It was our honeymoon. Besides, Paris is only an hour away. Bede understands. He always does." She spoke more to herself than to him. "Ready? We could run." Rocking on her heels, impatient, she reached out to him.

"I'm not dressed to run."

"Honey, I doubt that anyone will recognize you between here and the monastery."

"You never know."

"Okay. Even if someone does recognize us, you look handsome. I, on the other hand, am a mess."

He held her hand and began walking. "Your kind of famous is different from my kind of famous."

"Oh, really?"

"You're a mathematician. You're expected to look a mess."

"Oh, my God!" She snatched her hand away from his grip and stopped walking.

"Calm down! We can't afford to get separated." He reached out his hand.

"I'm not a child." She folded her arms.

"Then don't act like one! We need to get going." He continued his walk at a fast pace.

She ran to him and slipped her arm into his. "Did you enjoy Paris?"

"Well, let's see. I had the most expensive and luxurious resort booked for our honeymoon, but my beautiful wife decides we will experience Paris as nomads—run from place to place, live on the streets and alleyways, no room, no bed. And, oh yeah, yesterday, she gets bitten by a venomous snake in a zoo enclosure. That was a most memorable five days."

"Well, I thought..." She decided not to say anything else. *He just needed more time to appreciate the experience.*

They pushed their way through pockets of pilgrims as they pressed toward the monastery. Bridget smiled at all the dancing, talking, praying, singing, gathering, and cooking. She hoped no one offered them food. It was a mild offense to turn down a food gift as a pilgrim.

"I guess we should run," Jeremy said. "Are you okay to do this?"

"I'm fine. You worry too much."

"If we get separated—"

"Meet at the entrance? I know. Come on!"

Holding hands, the duo started off at a steady pace, weaving through the crowds. The closer they got to the monastery, the denser the pockets of pilgrims became. In some places, Jeremy pushed people out of the way, leaving Bridget to apologize in his wake. She would've tried to go around dense pockets of pilgrims. Not Jeremy. She loved his decisiveness as he plowed through. She nestled closer to him as he fought through the crowds.

"Not too much farther to go!" he shouted between deep breaths.

Ten minutes later the couple, breathing heavily, rapped at the large wooden monastery door. It opened. Jeremy flashed his passport and a letter at the doorman, which the man scrutinized before letting them in and closing the door behind them.

"It's so quiet," Bridget said. "It is like heaven in here."

"It's certainly much cooler," Jeremy pinched at his shirt and shook it to cool himself. "I should change my shirt."

"We're here now. No one's going to take your picture."

"You never know." He looked at her. "You know, for someone so beautiful, you lack elegance. You should care more about your appearance."

Bridget's eyes opened in disbelief. She shook her head. "You know what? You are a pompous—"

"Sister!" Jeremy interrupted her to address one of the Sisters crossing the foyer. "I'm Jeremy Blade. Can you direct us to the cavern room?"

The Sister's eyes lit up. "Oh, sweet Lord. It's Dr. Jeremy Blade. Dr. Bridget Blade. It's such a pleasure—two flights down. You can take the elevator or the stairs." She pointed at a doorway leading to the staircase. "Your brother," pointing to Jeremy, "Padre Bede is down there already." Her hands were trembling. "I'm so excited. We were going to ask you three to remain with us a few days, but I'll let Sister Kaypore talk to you. I really must run. The sun's going to... the miracle's going to happen any minute now."

"How can you tell, Sister? Can you share that with us?" Bridget stepped forward, her eyes alight with interest.

The Sister grabbed Bridget's hand with vigor. Letting go, she smiled, gathered up her habit, and scurried away.

"Well, you heard her, we should—" Jeremy started toward the elevator, but Bridget whipped past him to the stairwell. "Bridget?" He raced to follow her.

The rhythmic patter of their footsteps, punctuated by the periodic shuffle on the landing between the floors, filled the stairwell with a deafening echo. "I think I see it!" Bridget, the faster of the two, called out from beyond the bottom of the stairwell. Her footsteps signaled that she had broken into a sprint down the hallway, leaving Jeremy to chase after her yet again.

The automatic outer glass doors to the cavern room opened up, revealing a second set of doors. They helped each other remove their backpacks as they tried to catch their breath. A series of beeps cut through their frantic activity and the second set of doors opened, revealing a tall, smiling cleric—her brother-in-law.

"Hi, guys!" His excited voice filled the foyer.

Bridget jumped into his waiting arms, hugged him tightly, and then kissed his lips. She pulled back, ruffled his hair and laughed. "Bede, I'm so sorry we're late." She held his face in both hands. "We pretty much ran through all of Paris. We just kept moving. I'm sorry. I smell like a pig, don't I?"

He laughed, holding her hands. "Your honeymoon, five years late. Don't apologize."

"Hey, brother." He and Jeremy enveloped each other in a powerful hug.

Jeremy rubbed his brother's back. "Thank you for taking point on this."

"You both deserved the time alone together. Time away from me can be healthy," he said. "I missed you both so much."

Bridget punched Jeremy playfully in the arm. "Well, if it's any consolation, he talked about you quite a bit. Maybe next time you two should go on some kind of honeymoon!" They all laughed.

"I'm so happy you're here," Bede said. "I hope I set up everything correctly."

"I'm sure you did great," Jeremy said. "Let's get going!"

Bede led them further into the large room, an enormous hall built next to the massive cavern that wove through the base of the hill, up its spine, and opened on the back side. A large glass wall separated the room from the cavern.

"Every scientific team here is registered, fees paid up, waivers signed. Sister Lacey has been wonderful in providing everything we need." Bede pointed to clusters of equipment with scientific teams gathered around them. "Say hi," he said playfully.

Some of the other groups waved at them and a few gave the thumbs-up sign, clearly grateful for Jeremy's intervention in getting permission to set up equipment in the monastery.

"What a relief," Bridget said, as they pushed their backpacks into the corner of a large walk-in closet. She turned in a circle, observing the hall. "Bede," she whispered, "are there radioactive substances here? I thought we made that clear in the application process—nothing radioactive. There're people up there!"

"You don't miss much, do you? I'm sorry," Bede said. "Yeah, some of these guys did not follow the guidelines—rare opportunity and all. They brought all kinds of equipment, including—"

"You should've turned them away," she said. "Being here is a privilege. We—"

"Bridget, it's okay," Jeremy said.

"I screwed up," Bede said. "I just couldn't say no to all these people who'd transported all this equipment. Sister Kaypore was not happy, but she was gracious. So we installed the plastic lining around the room. There was no time to get lead panels, and besides, structurally, that would be difficult. We have a few lead aprons and a radiation suit. We pray nothing happens, but if it does, we'll take beta over gamma."

THE CLAY QUEEN

"Bede, you did a fantastic job," Jeremy said, glaring at Bridget. "We weren't here to help, so we certainly have no right to criticize your decisions."

"I wasn't criticizing him," Bridget responded. "I—"

"Where's the setup for the telescope?" Jeremy interrupted her.

"Since we'll be looking directly at the sun, as Bridget insisted, I set up the telescope and viewer in the alcove at the far end." He started toward their end of the room, weaving through groups of scientists.

"Who are they?" Bridget pointed in the opposite direction at the dozen people seated on the tiered benches a few feet from the large glass wall which separated the room from the cavern. Unlike everyone else in the cavern room, they were intently focused on the cavern itself.

"Mostly scientists, some observers... that one's from the Vatican." Bede pointed discreetly at a graying man in a black, long-sleeved shirt on the observation deck. "I don't know who the others—"

A ripple of energy shot through the hall, followed by excited chatter. "The Miracle of the Sun has already started up there." Bede's eyes lit with wonder, as he leaned forward to view one of the television screens on the wall, screens filled with images of pilgrims jumping in jubilation and thousands of hands pointing upward.

Bridget pushed him toward the workstation. "What about the blue light? Where does it manifest?"

"In the cavern. It's what they're all waiting for." Bede pointed back at the observation deck. "The readings on this one will be phenomenal, a treasure trove of data. Exciting times, huh?" He hurried them to their corner of the room and turned a screen toward them. "Look at that! We've got data and it's coming fast!"

Jeremy pumped his fist in excitement. Bridget put her arm around his waist.

"Let's see what's coming in," Bede said.

Both men squeezed in front of the screen; Bridget leaned in behind them, all three mesmerized by the stream of numbers filling the screen.

Bede straightened up, turned to the side, and wiped his eyes in obvious relief. Bridget and Jeremy looked at each other. She took hold of Bede's shoulders.

"I wish you wouldn't put so much pressure on yourself. Your work is always exquisite. Look at that! Your equipment designs are always so clever and elegant." Pointing at the screen, she squeezed close to him. "You should be proud. This is why we're always steps ahead of everyone else."

Bede beamed with pride, accepting a pat on the back from his brother.

"Hi." A breathless voice interrupted them. They all turned toward the greeting. Standing two feet from them was a pale woman with a broad smile and sparkling eyes. "I hope I'm not interrupting. I'm Kate Selz, *Le Monde*. May I get a comment from one of you?" She was short, which forced her to look up to make eye contact with the tall trio.

Bede pointed to one of the large monitors on the wall, which displayed an infrared image of the pulsating sun. "Not now, Kate. Later, I promise."

Kate turned to look at the television monitor providing ongoing live coverage of the pilgrim experience on the grounds above. "Padre Bede," she turned back to the three, "just a quick word. As a priest and engineer, why do you think...?" All three were already refocused on their computer monitor, engrossed in conversation.

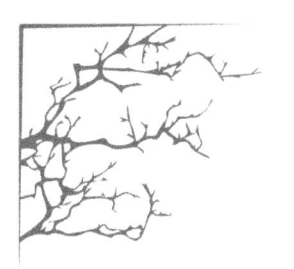

Chapter 5

"BEDE, YOU ARE AMAZING!" Bridget inspected one of the three telescope viewing chairs Bede had designed and set up in the dark corner alcove. "You did this in five days?"

Bede smiled. Her approval was important to him. He peeked out from behind the curtain within the alcove to check on Jeremy, who was reviewing the data coming from all the sensors scattered around the monastery grounds. "It was straightforward, and I had help. After everyone's initial set up, we were all hanging out with little to do. So I pressed all the Sisters and Brothers and these guys out there into service."

Bridget sat in a chair and grinned as it automatically adjusted to fit her body. "Is this for the viewing helmet?" She pointed at a green switch on the armrest. He nodded as he walked over and pulled down the helmet, which was attached to a retractable mechanical arm.

She got off the chair and walked around one of the telescopes. "This is a far more stable mount than I'd suggested—you reconfigured the imaging train. I like it," she said as she pressed on the truss nodes. She slid her slender fingers into the mechanisms of the guide scope and peered inside, taking a few moments to study it. "You're amazing. I'll never tire of saying it. I don't know how you clear your mind and sort out all these processes in such a short time. You are the most remarkable man I know."

He motioned her over and punched at keys on a computer attached to the wall. "Do you want to double-check your code for the ocular calibration?'

She shook her head. "I trust you. You know I hate looking over my work."

"How are you?" Bede asked.

"I'm fine... a little sad. We'll fill you in when we're done with all this." She made up the distance between them with a couple of steps and hugged him tightly. "I love you so much. We really missed you." She clung to his neck.

"Did something happen between you two?" Bede asked.

"When does something *not* happen between us? He's angry at me. It makes me feel so rotten when he's in this mood."

"He doesn't seem angry, and you seemed happy—you always seem happy, I suppose."

"Happy to see you. Besides, he gets angry if I'm sad or depressed."

"What happened? Did you make someone do something crazy?"

She winced at his displeasure. "Yes. And I think he'll need to vent." She pulled back enough to look into his face. "Don't ask him, please. Let him tell you when he's ready, okay? I love Jeremy with all my heart, but five days alone with him was more than I could handle. I needed a buffer. I needed you."

Bede chuckled. "Well, you always said you got two for the price of one, right?"

She smiled as she let go. "You're right. That was the deal. I married Jeremy on the condition that you were part of the package. He's happiest when you're around and is such the angel around you. He loves you more than he'll ever love me."

Bede stared at her for a few moments. "To be honest, it was awful with you gone. I felt so empty."

She reached out and held his hand. "Well, we've checked the box on the honeymoon. It's done and over with and I had fun. There is now no reason for the three of us to be separated ever again. Deal? Till death do us part?"

THE CLAY QUEEN

"Till death do us part!" He smiled. "Let's go see what my brother's up to."

THE MIRACLE OF THE Sun had begun and would likely continue for another forty-five minutes. The wall television screens displayed excited pilgrims pointing skyward. The data from the monitoring stations that Bede had set up around the grounds above were coming in just as they'd hoped. There were no hiccups so far. It was Bridget's task to interpret the numbers, but for now, that could wait.

Drained from the adventures of the past few days, she closed her eyes and stretched backward to relieve the tension in her body. Jeremy would have been furious with her if they'd missed any of this because of her insistence on honeymooning.

She smiled as she watched him, relaxed and relieved, doing his favorite thing in the world—spending time with Bede. Though he was a media darling and a social hero, Jeremy's hard-driving personality did nothing to temper his reputation as a surly task master—an image that she considered unfair.

No one understood the burden he bore, how each morning she awoke in a panic, only to be comforted by his kind, patient words. No one, but Jeremy, understood that the world made no sense to her. That the world was far too stable, and change happened slowly, if at all. Successive moments followed from the previous ones in a logic that defied her, that paralyzed her. Only Jeremy understood and cared and loved her all the same.

No one understood the painful magnitude of a simple pin prick. "She's dramatic," they'd always say. Never Jeremy. He bore her pain, literally. Around him, she felt her pain lessen as she drove it into him. The cost? Her pain was his agitation, his fear, his aggression, his persistent anger. Whether he knew or understood the nature of this transaction she had no idea, but that he accepted her and her absurdities willingly—that was love.

His reservoir of joy, though hidden and difficult to access, ran deep and was worth the effort. His depth was her most cherished secret—something she'd never give up for anything. He was happy for the moment, and that was all that mattered. Unburdened, it was her time to experience the joy of a divine manifestation and not worry about the equipment, or the numbers, or what Jeremy was thinking.

She walked into the bathroom and checked the stalls for others. She was alone. Careful to avoid her face in the mirror, she lifted up her t-shirt and gasped. Long, dark-blue spidery veins full of venom crisscrossed her torso. She pulled her long sleeves back and looked in dismay at the veins straining at the surface, desperate to rid themselves of the foreign poison.

Pressing her palms against the counter to steady herself, she reflected on the real reason she'd come into the restroom—to gaze at her face for the first time in years. She was finally here at the Monastery of Light. If there was healing for her fracturedness to be found anywhere, it was here. The divine was whole and certain. She, on the other hand, embodied chaos and ontological absurdity.

On three. One. Two. Three.

She looked directly in the mirror and screamed. Clasping her hands in front of her face, she cried as she took in deep breaths.

"Who are you? What do you want?" she screamed at the mirror, her gaze fixed firmly downward. There was no response. Why would there be? The faces, the other "hers" in her eyes, never answered.

Dizzy and nauseated, she sat under the towel dispensers and poured out her frustration in sobs. "Jeremy!" Her call was weak and drowned out by her crying. She pulled up her knees and laid her head between them until her breathing settled. Head down, she wiped away the tear stains, dried her face, and left the bathroom.

THE CLAY QUEEN

She needed to be alone. Peering toward the glass wall and past it into the cavern, she started in its direction.

"Bridget?" Jeremy called out from the back of the room. "Bede's set up a viewing station in that alcove." He pointed behind him, toward a curtain covering an opening in the wall.

She wanted to be close to him. If he knew what she'd done in the bathroom, he'd drop everything and make sure she was okay. But she needed to grow up and be independent. "I know. I was just in there. Go on without me. I want to walk down that way first." She pointed and started toward the cavern. "I'll be back in plenty of time."

Jeremy's knotted forehead expressed his displeasure, but Bede's kind smile reassured her. She understood Jeremy's frustration. This was the first time they'd captured the sun-miracle phenomenon. Because they worked best together when they bounced ideas off each other, it was important that all three experience the phenomenon together. Their observations would be crucial to improving subsequent versions of their experiment setup.

"Dr. Blade? Kate Selz…"

Bridget turned to the reporter, who kept pace with Bridget's brisk steps. She wiped her cheeks, hoping she'd dried her face well. "Kate, I promise we'll have something for you after we interpret the data." She offered a sympathetic look without slowing down as she tugged on her shirt to ensure her torso was covered.

"I just need a quote for my deadline." She exhaled loudly. "I'm the only reporter down here in the bowels of the Monastery of Light with Bridget, Jeremy, and Bede Blade. You guys are rock stars! My editor will kill me if I simply report what everyone else does."

"You don't give up, do you?" Bridget asked, unable to resist Kate's flattery. "All right." Bridget lowered her voice as they arrived at the dimly lit observation area facing the large glass wall. She pointed at the cavern straight ahead—dark, foreboding, and mysterious. "There is a rumor, a persistent one, that whenever there's the Miracle of the Sun, it's accompanied by the manifestation of a blue light." She looked at the reporter, an earnest short woman with a disarming smile. "But there's no one, not one person, who will come forward and claim to have seen this light."

Kate looked at Bridget with interest. "Then why take it seriously? Why are all these people sitting here? Why aren't you watching the real miracle out there?"

Bridget nodded and smiled, as she strained to see through the glass. "That's just it. The rumors are persistent. And even though the claims I heard are all indirect and secondhand, there's enough there to be of interest." She lowered her voice even more. "Many, including the Vatican, think the Order and devotees of Ryna see this light but hide the fact. There's no incentive for them to be forthcoming with documented accounts of this blue light. The Order hates all this attention on the monastery. All that activity up there, the pilgrims and all that... it's by the Vatican's mandate, not the Order. Jeremy had to work hard to convince them to let scientists set up observations on the grounds, and the best he could do was get this space underground."

Kate stopped scribbling on her notepad. "But you and your husband and Padre Bede have succeeded in documenting the supernatural. Why not set up your equipment here in the cavern? You could settle this."

Bridget remained transfixed by the cavern and did not respond immediately. She sighed. "We depend on grants to build our equipment. I would do it, but it would be incredibly difficult and expensive. Besides, we need to listen to dozens of first-hand accounts to know what to measure, how to build the equipment and, equally as important, how to set it up." She turned to the cavern, squinting to see beyond the glass. "In this case, we would have to build supports into the cavern wall for our equipment and, as you can see, that would be very dangerous; navigating the wind currents in the shaft would be difficult. But again, to even get the investigation off the ground, someone has to talk—and no one's talking."

"Thank you so much for taking the time to talk to me," Kate said. "It's just been a frustrating few days. This is the story of a lifetime, but it's been impossible to get sources, quotes—no one will talk to me, maybe because I'm a young reporter... I feel so invisible."

"You are not invisible," Bridget said turning to the cavern. "I see you."

"May I ask a few more personal questions? Off the record?"

"Nothing's ever off the record," Bridget said.

"I promise. This is," Kate said, tucking her notebook in her bag. "What was The Academy like? For something so public, it is so secretive!" Her eyes glowed with interest. "It's like a cult!"

"It's not a cult," Bridget said, feeling defensive. "It is exclusive, but there is transparency. Every country that contributes students can review the program, and they do."

"I wrote a story on The Academy, as a freelancer. No one would publish it—not even the tabloids! That's the power of The Academy—no one dares cross it. 'The Academy; the garden of the elite.'" Kate took a deep breath as she reflected on the memory. "My piece talked about you three." She smiled in satisfaction as she pointed at Bridget. "You know, I've followed you three for a while now. It's why I'm here. I begged for this assignment when I heard the three of you were coming. They say you are the greatest mathematician The Academy's ever produced—that Padre Bede is an engineering savant. And we all know about Jeremy Blade. The great Jeremy Blade." She tilted her head and asked, "What's it like being married to him? It must be amazing."

Bridget laughed in response to Kate's adulation. "I am proud to be his wife."

"Oh, I'm so jealous. To be the sole object of Jeremy Blade's affections..."

Bridget laughed again. "When this is all over, you and I and Bede and Jeremy can go to dinner together. Or maybe you can take Jeremy to dinner and I can have dinner with Bede." She winked at Kate, who responded with a laugh, placing her hand on her heart.

"Oh, God, please don't tease me like that." Kate fluttered her hands in a mock swoon.

Bridget inhaled. "I need to get back to work, Kate. I'll talk to Jeremy and Bede about letting you shadow us and see what we do."

"You are the sweetest person. Thank you so much, Dr. Blade."

"Call me Bridget." She shook Kate's hand.

"Kate." The reporter's infectious smile captured Bridget.

"Kate, I haven't eaten all day. Do you have anything?" Bridget asked sheepishly. She was hungry, but it was more than that. She wanted Kate to give her something. Something for which she would be obliged to be grateful. Something for which she would be forced to repay.

"Of course," Kate replied, as she set her handbag on the floor and rummaged through it. "Cream crackers?"

"Yes!" Bridget smiled gratefully.

"Anything, anytime. Just ask." Kate smiled and walked back toward another group in the middle of the room.

Bridget watched Kate, admiring the ease with which she interacted with people. There were no strangers to her. *Such a beautiful soul.* Would Kate take her up on her offer for dinner? It would be good to make a friend; a girlfriend for a change. She turned back to the cavern and shivered as she felt a chill. She'd spent too much time away from Jeremy and Bede and needed to get back to them.

I'm coming, Sweetheart. I need just one quick look.

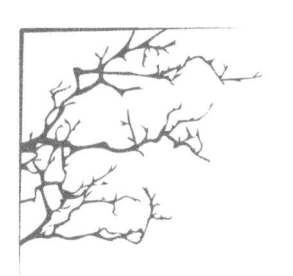

Chapter 6

BEDE AND JEREMY BOTH studied the checklist in front of them as Jeremy ran his finger down the crossed-out lines. "Everything looks good. Knock on wood, but it's been a good month."

"A few hundred million dollars richer," Jeremy said, swiveling back and forth on his chair. Prior to the honeymoon, Jeremy had closed on a deal to sell the company all three of them had founded. They had figured out how to create three-dimensional enhanced reality composites that could be easily manipulated. Although it was still in the beta stage, their bidders were desperate for the technology. As much as Jeremy wanted to secure the optimal deal, Bede and Bridget were far more concerned with getting the technology into the most trustworthy hands. The payout could have been twice what they received, but Bede and Bridget were satisfied, which meant he had to live with the agony of the opportunity's lost income for the rest of his life.

Bede exhaled. "Our EMF poles are set, and the NASA data is coming through."

"Pretty darn expensive data," Jeremy said. "We could have gotten the same data for free."

"Yes, but weeks after the fact," Bede smiled. "What's the purpose of all that money if we don't spend it? Thank you for negotiating with NASA, by the way. I couldn't have waited three weeks for this."

"How did you get the spectrometers on the rock face?" Jeremy asked.

"The Order. They're something else. They have climbing gear, and Sister Kaypore arranged everything. The angle of capture is excellent." He paused and looked at the five screens in front of them. "We should be able to interlace our data of the sun's magnetic topology with the standard mapping. It'll be a complex map, but there'll be strong inferences we can draw at the end of the process."

"You wish Bridget would start on the numbers now, don't you?"

"I suspect you do, too." Bede chuckled.

"Where is she now?" Jeremy looked down the hall, straining to see Bridget.

"I'm sure she'll join us. Let's go see the sun." Bede nudged Jeremy in the direction of the alcove. "You seem worried." Bede turned on a dim light in the makeshift telescope room.

"Did she tell you she got bitten by a snake?"

Bede spun around. "What?" He shook his head in disbelief. "No wonder she didn't want to say anything." He grunted in exasperation. "When did this happen?"

"Yesterday afternoon—venomous, too."

"Why didn't you tell me this?" Bede rested both hands on his waist. "Where?"

"At the zoo. Bridget, being Bridget, made the curator of the reptile enclosure let her into the snake pen. She wanted to feed the snakes."

Bede shook his head in disbelief. "You let her do that?"

Jeremy looked away. "I wasn't with her at the time. I almost had a heart attack when I saw her in there."

"You can't leave her alone, Jeremy. She's too naïve—no sense of danger." Bede took a deep breath. "I'm sorry. I didn't mean to snap at you. I just worry." He laid his hand on Jeremy's shoulder. "She seemed fine. Is she okay?"

"She had a very bad skin reaction, chills, aches, but of course, this didn't stop her. Nothing does. I couldn't sleep at all last night. I had to keep waking her just to make sure she was alive."

"Did you identify the snake?" Bede asked. "Her body will adjust, but just in case, we need to synthesize an antidote."

"I convinced her to talk the curator into letting us take the snake with us." Jeremy chuckled at Bede's wide-eyed reaction. "We walked out with a snake in our bag. Imagine that."

"Where is it now?" Bede asked.

"Get this. On the taxi ride, she decided it was too dangerous to have the snake while we were here; she said it was almost dead and that she was fine. So she threw it out of the window!"

"Did you identify it?"

"No. It was South American."

"Jeremy, that's not very helpful."

"I don't know," Jeremy said, exasperated. "Green with yellow spots; about a meter long with ugly eye slits. Its underbelly was yellow, as was the bottom half of its head. Does that help?"

Bede shook his head and rubbed his temples.

"She doesn't understand why I get so angry at her when she does these things," Jeremy said. "She's ridiculous! We spent five days running from place to place, sleeping in alleyways and common areas. That was her idea of fun. I suppose I'll look back someday and appreciate our... non-traditional honeymoon."

Bede shook his finger at his brother. "This is the last time I ever leave you two alone." He stood staring at Jeremy with his hands on his hips. "I was excited to show you this, but..."

"Don't let this get you down. She's fine."

"Well," Bede began, walking toward the telescopes and their viewing chairs. "Here's the setup. You sit in the chair, it adjusts to your specifications, the helmet viewer descends and connects to the telescope." He pushed a button and two of the chairs pulled out toward them. He helped Jeremy into his chair. "Now, fit your hands into the hand controls. They're like gloves. Right. Now you have remote control over the scopes, the cameras, and the focusing systems. Give it a shot while I get situated here." He then mounted his own chair. "Okay, here we go. We'll see if it works like it's supposed to."

The next few moments were filled with the brothers, hands raised like orchestra conductors, adjusting the telescopes for viewing.

"Now, stop for a moment. I'm going to activate Bridget's ocular calibrations. Bright flashes, but they should be fine." A series of clicks reverberated in the small room, followed by a series of rapid and very bright flashes directly into their eyes.

"Did you fiddle with the filters? The flashes are too bright," Jeremy said.

"Sorry. Just remain still a few more seconds," Bede called out. "There. We're all set. Here comes the sun!"

Both men gasped.

"Look at that! It's spinning. The sun is actually spinning," Jeremy whispered in reaction to twin orbs dancing around each other in his viewing scope. "What do you think it is? I definitely see two suns dancing around each other. An illusion? Clearly, the sun's not actually splitting into two spheres."

"It's something, isn't it?" Bede replied. "Well, we'll see from the data if there are any density or atmospheric distortions creating this illusion. I wonder what the satellites will pick up."

"Bridget's missing this," Jeremy said, unable to suppress his irritation.

"She's fine. She'll be here soon. I'm sure," Bede responded. "This is a sealed, confined space—no snakes, mushrooms, bacteria-filled pools. She can't possibly get into any mischief."

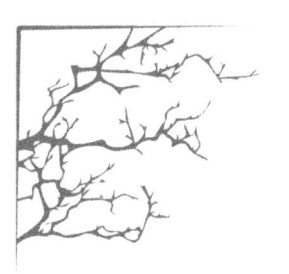

Chapter 7

BRIDGET STEPPED UP to the side of the observation benches. They looked like gymnasium stands, giving the space an auditorium-like feel. The glistening cavern walls, wet from the constant drip of water seeping through the rock, made it very difficult to sort out what was beyond the glass wall. Overwhelmed by the sheer vastness of the cavern, she retreated for a moment and pressed herself against the stands. She felt an intense desire for solidarity to combat the isolation the cavern evoked in her. She looked over at all the observers to her right; all staring intently toward the cavern, yet focused on different areas. The only person not transfixed was the graying man from the Vatican, who seemed to watch everyone else with calculated scrutiny. He locked eyes with her. She immediately turned away, looking downward.

She returned her focus to the faintly-lit cavern and forgot about the man and the other observers. Taking a deep breath, aware that she was breaking protocol, she strode to the glass wall for a closer look. Pressing the side of her face against the glass, she looked downward. Her view was obstructed by the terrace on the other side of the glass. She looked over to the left side, tracing her view upward until she couldn't see any further. She then followed an imaginary line at the top and to the right.

She gasped. *What is that?*

There was a small blue light up toward the right corner of her viewing frame. She raised tingling fingers to her chest to calm her thumping heart. She turned around to the observation deck. Thankfully, no one was watching her. She turned back, but the light was gone.

Desperate to see the light again, she looked further down the glass wall to her left—and at the far end was a door. Keeping her gaze firmly at the spot where she initially saw the light, she shuffled sideways until she felt the door with her left hand. She opened it discreetly and stepped out onto the landing.

The swirling air currents pushed her hard against the glass, snapping her neck backward against the viewing glass wall. *Oh, Bridget! You're an idiot! There's a reason no one's allowed out here!* She leaned her back flat against the glass for stability. In contrast to the air-conditioned interior, the air out here was damp, musty, and humid. The smell was unpleasant and intense, but she welcomed its naturalness.

Wow! The size of this thing! She estimated the cavern was about forty feet across. There was a short railing and a long way down into darkness. Above her, far beyond what she could discern with the naked eye, she knew that the cavern veered left and took a winding path to the surface on the other side of the hill.

Keeping her back against the glass wall to steady herself, she removed her lead apron and goggles, waited for her eyes to adjust to the ambient illumination, and stared at the rock wall opposite her.

There you are!

The light, an intense translucent blue, barely larger than a candle flame, hovered just in front of the rock. Her skin rippled with goose bumps as she leaned against the glass and slid into a sitting position, never taking her eyes off of it.

"What are you?" she whispered.

As though in response to her voice, the light flickered ever so slightly. With the flicker, she felt a rush from her stomach up into her chest, a burning sensation, causing her to vomit. She coughed out a harsh acidic fluid. Her body roared to life in a way she'd never felt. It was like turning on all the lights.

Every single cell seemed to charge up, sending a jolt of electricity through her, back and forth, until it subsided a few seconds later. Her heart beat hard against her chest and her body throbbed. Lightheaded, she waited for the spinning to stop and then closed her eyes to orient herself. The moment was over and she tried to catch her breath.

"What are you?" She groaned as she opened her eyes. The light, a blue flame, flared and swelled to the size of a baseball in response to her voice. She screamed as her body reacted again to the light. Her stomach knotted in violent cramps as she heaved. "No! Please!" she called out. In response, she felt fierce, fiery waves wash through her. The flame flared again at the sound of her voice. "No! no!" she pleaded, but to no avail. The flame, as if in response, intensified. The light flared brighter. *Oh, no! It's coming closer!*

"Help!" Bridget yelled in despair as the buffeting winds drowned out her raspy call. Her body burned internally and her skin felt like it was liquefying.

The light approached, expanding as it got closer. The nearer it got, the more she could sense something. *Intent?* Overcome by an overwhelming curiosity, she fought off the pain and pushed up onto her knees. The world rocked back and forth as she steadied herself. She heard muted thumps and looked toward the glass, but saw only blackness beyond. Disoriented and terrified, she couldn't think of why Jeremy wouldn't come to help her. She turned back to the light and screamed in shock. The blue light had traversed the width of the cavern and was now as large as she was, hovering just in front of her.

It was the most beautiful thing she'd ever seen, a very large, diaphanous, translucent bubble, swirling with colors, and with a radiant blue interior. *There's something alive in there!* The pain no longer mattered. Consumed by an all-encompassing desire to see into this bubble, she concentrated her gaze on its interior. And there it was, a smallish, thin, blue, glowing… creature?

"Hello?" she called out softly. The light flared again, searing her all over.

"Nouei!" a distant voice replied. It came from the creature, but sounded like a call from a distance, full-throated but faint.

"Noo-aye?" Bridget repeated the word. At the sound of her voice, the light flared even brighter. Her body felt like a fully-lit furnace, but she was too transfixed by this creature to succumb to the pain.

"You're so far away. I can't see you," the distant voice returned. "Are you there?"

"Noo-aye? What does that mean?" Bridget's speech was slurred; she tried to maintain control of her tongue.

"I can feel you, but I can't see you, my love," the voice said.

"You can't see me, can you... *my love?*" Bridget replied. There was an explosive flash. The light advanced and was white hot, the creature within much bigger.

"I miss you so much, my love. I must leave now." The distant voice faded in.

"No!" Bridget reached out but the light, a vehicle for the creature, retreated just out of her range. She shifted her weight slightly and pivoted closer to the light. It did not want to be taken. She could sense it, but she just could not let it leave. With a fluid and fast motion, she plunged her hand into the light and made contact. *There, I've got you.* "I have you now. Can you see me?"

The creature seemed panicked and confused. It fought to release itself, thrashing back and forth. "No, no, it's okay... my love?" Bridget spoke calmly.

The creature stopped as though it heard something. For the first time, it looked at her. Its eyes sparkled, accentuating its radiant smile. Bridget, captivated, let go, releasing one of its wrists slowly and letting her fingers brush against the creature's hands.

"My love, my Theresa. It's you! You made it!" The creature spoke with the distant voice.

Bridget's body tingled with a rush of intense affection for the bluish, bald humanoid female. "My middle name is Theresa. How did you know that? Who are you? What is a Noo-aye?" Bridget released her fingers and let go of the woman's other arm.

"Nouei, you're fading, I can no longer see you. I must go, my love!"

"No!" Desperate for the creature's affection, Bridget instinctively grabbed both of its arms again. The creature fought to free itself but couldn't.

What am I doing? Let her go!

Sensing that the being was weakening, Bridget released her grip. The creature looked at her curiously and then smiled again in recognition. It looked around, obviously confused, and then back to her. Without warning, the being plunged into her. She felt no immediate sensation. Then something stirred in her. It felt like a spinning ball of molten lava. She clutched her chest in horror as the fiery ball exploded inside her. She screamed and blacked out.

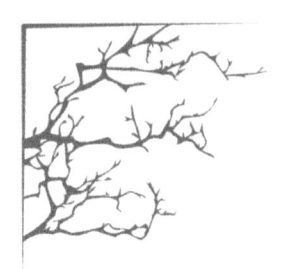

Chapter 8

"WHAT IS THAT?" BEDE said as he removed his helmet and eyepiece.

"Sounds like static," Jeremy replied.

Both stayed quiet as they concentrated on the crackling sound just outside the alcove.

"It's the Geiger counter," said Jeremy, his panic apparent. Both men jumped out of their chairs, through the curtain and back to their workstation.

"Not good!" Jeremy muttered. "Where's Bridget?"

"Blade!" another scientist called out. "Are you getting this?"

"Yes! Lock the place down!" Bede called out. "Radiation emergency!"

A woman from one of the other research teams raced to the entrance, smashed the glass protecting the lockdown controls and pulled the large red lever down and to the side, locking it in place. A shrill siren pierced the entire floor, followed by a calm, mechanical female voice. "Lockdown in sixty seconds."

"Bridget!" Jeremy called out. "Bridget!"

Bede ran to the supply closet and returned with a large box. "Here, take this quickly." He handed a few capsules to Jeremy before hurrying to distribute them.

"Bridget?" Jeremy called out again as he rushed toward the observation deck. "Ms. Selz! Ms. Selz! Have you seen my wife, Bridget Blade?" He stopped at the edge of the observation deck, handing her a capsule.

"Yes, she's out there, on the external viewing area." She pointed toward the glass wall. "What is this?"

"Ferric Ferrocyanide. Why is she out there?" He started toward his wife, but Kate gripped his forearm.

"Should I take this too? Someone gave it to me. I don't know what it is." She held up a yellow-colored capsule.

He swatted the capsule from her hand. "Potassium Iodide, I think. That's not going to help you. It could harm you. Help me with Bridget."

Pushing against the rush of people, they got to the glass wall.

"Dammit, I can't see anything," Jeremy said, pressing his nose against the glass.

"That thing's really crackling," she said, pointing at the Geiger counter.

"The radiation's concentrated in there. There she is. Bridget!" He pounded on the glass at Bridget, who was lying on the floor of the landing on the other side of the glass wall. She was moving, but something was clearly wrong.

Bede caught up to them with the radiation suit half on. "The radiation has decreased in that end of the hall, but it's increasing here." He struggled to get the suit on.

Jeremy banged repeatedly on the glass. "Bridget! Bridget! What is she doing there?"

Bede ran to the door. Jeremy pulled up a chair, stood on it, and in a quick violent motion, yanked on the weighted bar above the door, breaking it. "It'll shut quickly this way."

Bede nodded. He lifted a finger and then, with Bede patting his hand on his forearm, they both counted. "One, two, three!" On the third count, Bede swung the door open and stepped out.

"Ten seconds! Bring her in!" Jeremy yelled as he swung the door shut.

He remained by the door and strained to watch Bede, who tried to break into a run. Bede's body lit up with sparks. He raised his arms as though to protect himself but a wind current caught him, midstride and unbalanced, smashing him against the glass wall. He attempted to steady himself, taking a shaky step toward Bridget before buckling to the ground—motionless.

The door clicked. Jeremy tugged on it furiously. It didn't budge.

"It's the lockdown," Kate said in desperation. "Everything's sealed. Can we delay the lockdown by a few seconds?"

Jeremy stared in shock through the glass. "We have to get them out of there!"

"Blade! Stand back!" Before he could take any action, two sets of hands yanked him away from the door as a thick reinforced door descended, sealing off the room.

BEDE GROANED AS HE slowly regained consciousness. His head pounded, but there was no way to touch it through his suit. He rotated his torso gingerly until he was on his back and took a few deep breaths. *Jeremy? Bridget!*

He rolled over to his knees but fell hard on his side. He flipped over on his back and took a few moments to muster his strength. He forced himself onto his stomach. Propped up on his forearms, he waited. He felt the strain on his shoulders and realized he was weakening but didn't know why. He had to act quickly.

He lifted himself on all fours and waited to steady himself, his loud breaths filling the suit.

Something's wrong. Something's wrong. Drop!

A blinding flash illuminated the cavern, followed by a booming, static, crackling sound. Trembling, he lifted his head slowly and looked straight ahead. There was something just ahead of him. It was Bridget, splayed out on the landing, visible in the residual fading flashes.

"Bridget! Bridget!"

There was no response. Another blinding flash erupted, plunging the cavern into blackness. The installed lights had burned out.

He waited until his eyes adjusted enough to trace shadow-like forms. Summoning all his strength, he slithered toward Bridget, bumping into her feet with his arm. Surprised, he looked at what he had bumped into but there was nothing there but a pure black outline of feet. He followed the dense black outline of her body in confusion. She was so intensely black that she seemed like a hole in the darkness.

"What happened, Bridget?" he muttered.

He ran his fingers up her leg and realized that her clothes were mostly gone, burned off. His arms ached from the exertion. He lowered his head to rest his neck for a few moments. Returning his gaze to Bridget, he gasped in fright as the outline of Bridget's body gradually changed color, glowing and flickering untill it became a bluish light. Her body flickered with the strange color before reverting back to the pure blackness.

"Bridget!" he called, but there was no response. No movement. Waves of panic flowed through him as the helplessness of his situation dawned on him. The swirling winds howled like forgotten souls. He refused to consider the fact that she might be dead. *She'd survived so much already. Why not this?*

The darkness defining her body receded until she was now a shadow. He leaned in close. *Oh, God!* Her arm closest to him was singed and blistered. He pulled himself up and studied her, observing in dismay burns all over her body. His suit, though equipped with audial amplifiers, could not pick up any breathing. But that did not mean that she was dead. There were too many sounds echoing in the cavern to pick up faint breathing. He laid a gentle hand on her chest and thought he felt the chest cavity expand and contract. There was still a soul in there, he hoped as he stroked a singed remnant patch of hair gently, careful not to put pressure on her skin. He was spent. He was too late and the lockdown was in place. But Jeremy was on the other side—he would come. *He'll figure something out,* he thought. He laid down with his head facing hers and closed his eyes in exhaustion.

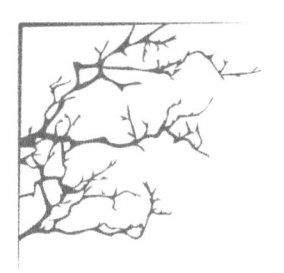

Chapter 9

JEREMY STRUCK THE REINFORCED door separating him from his brother and his wife. Exhausted, he rested his forehead on the wall.

The radiation levels in the cavern were far too high, and at this point it was likely that he'd lost one or even both of them. Forever.

"Mr. Blade?" Kate said his name as she laid her hand gently on his shoulder. "You need to see this."

He kept his gaze on the lead wall, almost certain there was a way through.

"Mr. Blade!" Kate's voice rang louder. "There's something going on up there." She pointed upward.

"What?"

Kate came into view as he turned. His voice cracked, forcing him to clear his throat.

She pointed to one of several large screens in the room. "I think our lockdown does not matter," she said.

Still leaning on the partition, he watched the television monitor. Then he looked at Kate, confused.

She shook her head. "People started getting sick. It set off a panic... ten thousand people..."

The television images focused on panic-stricken pilgrims pushing, running, stomping, and crushing each other. What appeared to be lost children wandered through the frantic crowds. Blood-stained pilgrims pleaded for help. Empty upturned wheelchairs lay about. An unsteady camera attempted to capture the moment.

"Any dead?" he croaked, as he tried again to clear a lump in his throat.

"I had counted at least a dozen, possibly…" Kate's voice trailed off. "This is a disaster." She covered her trembling lips with her hands, her eyes remaining fixed on the screens.

Jeremy closed his eyes for a few moments and steadied himself. There was nothing he could do for Bridget or Bede. Bede had a full body suit on and might possibly survive, but it was over for Bridget. If she ever regained consciousness, she would die in a day or two.

He looked up at the screen, filled with images of a hysterical mob. This was a situation that could be fixed, and he could fix it.

He rubbed his hand against the partition and kissed it for a few moments, uttering a silent prayer. Motioning to Kate to follow him, he walked toward the center of the room and clapped his hands to get the attention of everyone there. After the screens were muted he said, "If there are no objections, I am going to override the lockdown. We can do more out there than in here."

He looked around at the faces focused on him. People nodded in silence. There were no vocal objections. He walked over to a console by the door, pulled out a manual from a shelf under the keypad, and entered the override key. A shrill tone signaled the end of the lockdown, followed by clicks. The lead wall partitions enclosing the glass wall and the entrances would each still have to be unlocked manually.

"We'll need two groups. One group will remain down here to clean up and create space. We'll need this as a staging area for the injured." He faced the people to the left side of his vision. "I'll need another group to come up with me. We need to go up there."

He left the rest unsaid. With a decisive sweep of his arm, he divided the group in two. "You all, come up with me. Kate, you're with me. The rest of you, remain here."

"What about them?" a man called out, clearly referring to Bede and Bridget.

"The radiation levels are still too high in the shaft. It is better…" he paused, unable to complete his sentence.

A man walked up from the rear of the group. "Blade, you go ahead. We will help them. Bede has on the only radiation suit down here, but there be another in storage somewhere upstairs. We'll find a way to get them out. You go up and take care of them." He pointed upward.

Jeremy managed a grateful smile. "Thank you." With singular focus, he raced through the door with his group.

JEREMY BOUNDED UP FIVE flights of stairs, absorbed in the task ahead. He emerged from the stairwell into a large entrance lobby filled with dozens of agitated Brothers and Sisters. The Order of Ryna, exceptionally reserved and private, were wholly unaccustomed to dealing with the public, much less a catastrophe such as the one unfolding beyond the doors. The lobby quieted as the desperate expectant gazes settled on him, grateful to have a favorable advocate of Jeremy's stature.

He hastened to the large wooden entrance door, peeked out, and then shut it as quietly as he could. Thankfully, someone had thought to lock the gates leading to the door, which had kept people away from the monastery itself. He gave himself a moment to plan as he positioned himself in view of everyone present.

"I need a liaison; someone I can communicate with." He scanned the foyer.

One of the Sisters responded. She was a tall woman with a regal bearing, made all the more compelling by her flowing white habit and gold-trimmed scarf. "I'm Sister Vesta Kaypore. Dr. Blade, we've communicated by phone, but it is an honor to finally meet you in person." She held his hand and spoke tentatively. "Is your wife... here?"

Jeremy swallowed. There were tasks to be accomplished and no time to dwell on matters beyond his control. "She's downstairs."

She smiled. "I look forward to seeing her."

He took a deep breath. "We'll need a staging area for information, coordination, lost children, and general logistics."

"Understood," Sister Kaypore responded.

"We'll need an infirmary. I suggest we use the hall downstairs, but this is your monastery, and if you have better ideas, then go for it."

Sister Kaypore nodded vigorously.

Satisfied, he paused and looked around at the nervous gazes. "We're going out there. We have to be strong, decisive, and we have to bring calm to that chaos. Everything you do from now on is to limit the damage to Ryna's honor. She will be blamed for this. We have to make it clear that this has nothing to do with the sun miracle or any other natural manifestation of Ryna."

He lifted his head; his chin slightly elevated. "We are heartbroken! That's what the world needs to see." His vibrant gestures communicated as much as his words. "I understand that the Order is reclusive, reserved, stoic. To you, these are virtues. To the world, it's aloofness. This can't be the face you show the world. Not now." He sighed, sensing everyone's distress. "Convey Ryna's love. Let them see that she is heartbroken. Let the world see that you care, and that *you* are heartbroken. Let them see your hearts!" Notwithstanding the trepidation in their eyes, he sensed resolve and agreement.

He pointed to the group he had brought with him from the subterranean level of the monastery. "Brace yourselves. There are going to be hundreds of dead, trampled people. The last thing we need is a pile of dead bodies in the pavilion outside the Monastery of Light. All the dead must be taken to the back compound, and all media devices must be restricted, how ever you can. We can always apologize or replace equipment. You can never take back haunting images of stacks of dead people associated with the monastery or Ryna."

"But how do we know who's dead and who's not?" someone asked.

Jeremy thought for a moment. "Use your best judgment. Having hundreds of dead or unconscious bodies sprawled outside the monastery is a non-starter. Image is everything, and our priority is to protect Ryna's honor." Protecting Ryna's honor was not actually important to many of these scientists, but that didn't matter. He hoped everyone understood the need for order and calm, both now and in the near future. Given recent religious tensions, it would do no good to allow this tragedy to be laid at the feet of a religious sect.

He turned toward the door and heard a loud commotion behind him. The Brothers and Sisters were leaving. Confused, he called out to them. "Wait, where are you going?"

Sister Kaypore stepped forward. "Dr. Blade, these aren't our work habits. These are ceremonial habits that we wear on occasions such as today."

"No, don't change," Jeremy took steps to place himself in the middle of the group.

"But they're white and delicate material, not suitable for hard work. We can accomplish a lot more if we change."

"I agree that you can accomplish more, *comfortably*. But I want the world to see you in your beautiful, majestic, and blood-stained habits. It's the visual we need."

Not waiting for a response, he walked toward the door in the hope that they would follow. At the front door he turned to Kate. "I need you to convince one of those camera crews to work with you. I will make calls and get them a privileged feed on one of the networks. I want every shot to have a Sister or Brother helping or grieving. No shots of the dead."

Kate looked at him, her lip quivering. He knew she was trapped between her natural compassion and her journalistic obligations.

"Kate? Are you with me on this? There are dead people out there. This is no time to be a journalist. All you are, in this moment, is a human being."

She took a deep breath and gave him a barely perceptible nod. He scanned the lobby. Satisfied, he opened up the door.

"Come on. Let's get out there!"

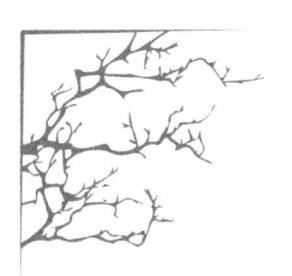

Chapter 10

JEREMY ACHED FROM ALL the lifting, dragging, and carrying of the past hour. It felt good to stand up straight for a moment, relax his shoulders, and stretch.

Above the tree line, the day was still a beautiful one. The sky was a brilliant blue, soothing the eyes until they returned to the carnage below, the result of a panicked mob. As expected, many casualties included the weakest—children and the elderly. But the most gruesome injuries were indirect and far less discriminating. Thousands of pilgrims had been pinned by the throngs against stone benches, trees, and walls.

Jeremy crouched to inspect the lifeless body of a young man at his feet. The man's head hung unnaturally from his body. His broken arms were splayed, and his knees curled up to his stomach. Jeremy lifted the victim's ripped t-shirt and examined his badly-bruised torso. He touched the corpse's hair and traced along its jawline. He tried in vain to close the eyes, but they stared blankly.

"You'd think the young, strong ones would have survived." Kate's deep voice snapped him back into the present. "You wonder what his story was."

Jeremy stood up and took a deep breath.

"Are you okay, Jeremy?" She reached up and placed her hand on his shoulder. He nodded, still struck by the corpse's utter lack of vitality. "I just came up from the cavern room. A few radiation suits will be here soon."

"Thank you for the news."

"You look worried and exhausted. Do you really want to do this interview?"

He nodded. "It's important."

"Okay. I've co-opted these guys," she added, pointing to a camera crew a few feet away. "Jeremy, I'm going to have to ask some pretty direct questions."

"That's fine."

Kate surveyed the scene. "So, give me some background before we begin. What happened here? Was it the sun?"

"I don't know," he said. "It couldn't have been the sun. Much too large. It would be impossible for the sun to have had such a localized reaction. The sun-miracle phenomenon is not literally a sun phenomenon. It is a divine phenomenon."

"I don't understand."

"The activity of Ryna in this location creates the appearance of the pulsating sun, or the twin orbs, or the enlarged sun. There's nothing special about the sun per se in this location. The sun was definitely not the source of the radiation."

"Then what was?" she said.

"Have you been to the Caverne de Dieu? The entrance to the cavern under the monastery?"

"Yes. It's one of the most beautiful places on earth." Pointing to the woods half a mile away, she added, "It's on the other side of the hill, beyond those woods."

"Radiation was most intense in the cavern shaft. So it must have burst out of there, up through the cavern, through the woods, and to the pilgrims here. But there are reports that the effects were also felt in the other direction. It was isotropic. It radiated out from a single non-heat source, without residual radiation. I have no explanation yet." He paused as if he had more to say. "I am dying to solve this riddle, but haven't had much time and can't find our sensors. I thought I knew all the places Bede set up monitoring equipment, but I can't find anything. That data is crucial in making sense of all this."

Kate regarded him thoughtfully for a moment. Then, "Jeremy, that's far too complicated an answer for what we need. Save explanations for later. Right now, I need simple, declarative answers and a strong call to action." He nodded. "Okay. Ready to do this?"

"How do I look?" He straightened out his rolled-up sleeves.

"Very good, all things considered. You don't want to look too polished, not that it really matters. You do have a face for television." She smirked as she fixed his collar and straightened his shirt with smart outward strokes. "And how do I look? Be kind, I'm a print lady."

"Well, apart from the beads of sweat on your forehead, your flushed face, and your uneven hair, I would guess that the camera will be kind to you."

"Is there a compliment in there anywhere?" She allowed a small smile at his earnestness and slapped his arm playfully.

Jeremy watched Kate go over final instructions with her camera crew and then waited patiently as they moved him around for the best shot. Kate then stood next to him with a microphone, and the cameraman counted down with his fingers.

"I'm Kate Selz with *Le Monde*, here with an exclusive special report on this tragic, tragic day." She turned her face up into the steadfast gaze of Jeremy. "I'm here with Jeremy Blade, entrepreneur, inventor, and policy advisor. Thank you, Jeremy, for taking the time to talk with me."

He nodded but said nothing.

She continued, "You and I were deep down in the Monastery of Light, this beautiful, holy place behind us, when tragedy struck. In your expert opinion, what happened?"

"Thank you, Kate. As you know, my wife, my brother and I, along with many respected scientists and observers from around the world, were here to witness the Miracle of the Sun. Shortly after noon, a sudden and massive spike in radiation shot through the area. I must emphasize that the sun miracle has occurred every seven years for a century now without any such complication; this devastating radiation was utterly unconnected to the Miracle of the Sun."

"Then what was the source of the radiation—and are we safe?" She probed, stressing the last phrase.

"Yes, we are," Jeremy responded. "There appears to be no residual radiation. As you can see around us, the Sisters and Brothers of the Order are out here helping the sick and injured. We are all heartbroken," Jeremy gestured in the direction of the camera. "I appeal to you, come and help us. This is a time for us all to work together."

Kate laid her right hand on his left shoulder and oriented her figure toward the camera. "Mr. Blade." She made a well-practiced turn toward him. "Some would say it might be time to rethink the Rynean embrace of nature—that Ryna is an archaic god, and the transition to Thysia is long overdue. Isn't this event evidence that Ryna and her teachings belong to a bygone era?"

Jeremy looked off to the left. Her reference to Thysia had caught him off guard, and he needed to buy time. "Those of us who love and worship Ryna do not exclude Thysia. Ryna is Thysia. Even the Vatican would agree. Thysia is a more sophisticated theological representation of Ryna, but we do not worship different gods…"

She interrupted. "But hasn't the Vatican outlawed the worship of Ryna?"

"No. The rites and rituals of Ryna are no longer the standard form and have been removed from contemporary manuals, but the rituals themselves have not been banned." He paused, but continued before Kate could counter. "I grew up in a household that worshiped Thysia. I…" his gaze shifted beyond the camera. "I loved and married a wonderful woman who happened to worship Ryna, so I converted. My brother…" he interlaced his fingers, closed his eyes and swallowed. "My brother is even a priest of Thysia. But we are a happy, loving family. All of us are heartbroken today. Ryneans and Thysians lie here in pain, needing help. Please come to our aid, and put aside our so-called differences." He spoke earnestly, directly into the camera.

Kate also turned to the camera, keeping her hand on Jeremy's elbow. "This is a tragedy, but perhaps it can also be a moment of unity as we set aside our differences in pursuit of a common humanity. Dr. Jeremy Blade, I thank you for your time."

The cameraman counted down and then powered down. She squeezed Jeremy's upper arm. "You did very well."

"You didn't warn me about the Thysia question."

"Not everything can be scripted, you know? I knew you would have a good response. But it had to look genuine and not studied, so I surprised you a bit. It was very good." She watched him as he appeared to debate the value of fussing further. "Jeremy, we're on the same side. I wanted you to look strong, caring, and genuine, and we accomplished that."

"You did," he conceded. "Thank you."

"You seem agitated."

"I hate being helpless," he said.

"The process out here seems under control. Sister Kaypore can take over. We can go check on the progress with your wife and brother.

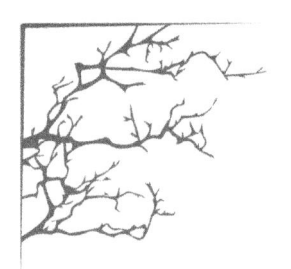

Chapter 11

CRIES AND SCREAMS FILLED the stairwell which led to the monastery's subterranean floors. Jeremy and Kate pressed themselves against the wall to allow the injured being helped down to the cavern room to pass by. Splattered blood dotted the stairs, tracing paths all the way down, and wet crimson handprints coated the handrails.

The corridor leading to the entrance of the hall was lined with more injured—the less urgent cases. There were too many injured, and not enough medical supplies. The few available medical staff and volunteers moved between huddled groups of injured, offering water and words of comfort.

Jeremy stopped to investigate a stack of boxes against a wall. A series of flashes startled him. He turned to Kate, who was scrolling through the pictures she'd taken.

"Something wrong?" she asked.

"Supplies have begun to arrive. These are sterile bandages, but there are no adhesives here, from what I can tell. You need both to get the best use out of them. Besides, I bet no one knows they're here." He sighed. "I know this is an emergency, but it's worth taking the extra time to plan; otherwise we get these logistical chokepoints and inefficiencies. With careful planning, all these people could be documented, treated, and attended to within three hours."

"Stay still!" A young voice filtered up from the floor.

Next to the stack of boxes were two boys, probably brothers, seated against the wall. One was cutting through the other's sleeves.

"Can I help you?" Jeremy crouched.

The boy nodded and handed the scissors to Jeremy.

Jeremy held out the boy's hand and inspected it while Kate crouched next to them. A series of clicks followed from her camera. He cut carefully through the sleeve, revealing dried blood and a series of bruises up the boy's arm.

The smaller of the two boys pulled out a large bandage and applied it to his brother's forearm. "Thank you, Mister!"

There was no point asking about their parents, especially if he couldn't offer immediate help. But they had each other and that was good for now.

"Jeremy? We have to go."

He joined Kate, and together they hurried through the door into the cavern hall. The large space, which had been filled with tables and equipment only an hour ago, was now strewn with hundreds of injured on thin mattresses or blankets. Desperate brothers, sisters, and medical professionals rushed between the wounded, whose cries of pain were far more intense in here than out in the corridor. The large industrial oscillating fans spaced through the hall did nothing to relieve the stifling conditions or the smell.

"Jeremy!" The call came from the cavern end of the hall.

Jeremy and Kate rushed over, weaving through the infirm and their providers. A large mobile partition had been set up to keep the sick separated from the rescue activity.

"We've got a radiation suit, but we have a different problem now." A woman pointed in the direction of the cavern. "There's a wicked electromagnetic field in there. We don't know the source. It's intense, but it's confined in the space beyond the glass—in the cavern itself."

"Odd. Any radiation?" Jeremy's gaze traced the temporary aluminum shield along the glass wall.

"All three types," she said. "But get this—the gamma stops a meter in on our side of the glass. I don't know what to make of it. We're rigging up a Faraday cage so we can go in there and get them. But Jeremy," the woman said, laying a hand on his shoulder. "I don't think—"

"We can't give up," Jeremy said, feeling lightheaded at the thought of life without either Bede or Bridget.

"Oh, no. We're not going to give up at all," she said. "I just don't want you to get your hopes up. Okay? Maybe you shouldn't be here." She patted him on the shoulder and hurried off to the team constructing the cage.

"Can you explain what exactly they're doing?" Kate asked, flipping a page in her notebook. "Would that stop the radiation?" She nodded her head in the direction of the thick fumes and sparks created by two welders working on the cage.

"They're constructing a Faraday cage. Something in the cavern shaft is generating an electromagnetic field. The Faraday cage would shield anyone who goes in from the electrical charges," Jeremy said, glancing at the people working on the cage. "But we have *two* problems now—radiation *and* electricity."

"Jeremy." Kate put away her notebook and held his hand. "Bridget and your brother may not—"

"Something's not right here," he said, pulling her toward the covered glass wall. He stood about a meter and a half from it. "According to her, the gamma radiation stops here, like there's a wall."

"What would cause that?" She reached out as though to touch the imaginary wall.

"Nothing," he replied. "Once created, it radiates out as fast as light, especially since there is a source generating it. The entire monastery grounds should be flooded with radiation."

"I don't understand." Kate looked at him. "Is there a field blocking the gamma rays? Are they building up behind this invisible wall?"

"I don't understand it, either," he said softly. He walked toward the door and stood in front of it, but at a distance. "I'm going in to get them."

Kate gasped and pulled at his hand. "Jeremy, don't!"

The alarm in Kate's tone stopped all activity around them. The welding, the arguing, the chatter—all stopped.

"Blade, what are you doing?" One of the engineers spoke up. "You don't have any protection... the cage is not ready. We're getting there. Give us a few minutes."

"I'm going in to get my brother and my wife. Hand me those gloves." He gestured to Kate.

She handed him a pair of thick brown gloves. "Jeremy, you can't go..." Kate pleaded, placing a soft hand on his elbow.

He raised his hand to silence the protests that had erupted. Turning to Kate's worried gaze, he reached down with his other hand and gave her hand a squeeze.

His breaths felt shallow, and the lightheadedness of previous moments returned. Bridget was the most unusual person he'd met. She always said nothing in nature could kill her. So far, she'd survived a venomous snake, poisonous mushrooms, a fire ant swarm three years ago—not to mention years prior when she'd been partially submerged in a hot spring with thermophilic bacteria. She suffered in all cases, but she never died. She controlled something about the forces of nature. There was nothing mechanical generating this EM field. As inexplicable as it was, it had to be naturally generated, which meant it wouldn't kill her. But if she had the power to keep herself alive, then why couldn't she keep him safe? If neither Bede nor Bridget was to live, neither would he.

"Bridget! Bridget, honey, I'm coming," he called out.

Jeremy pointed at the man with a Geiger counter who'd been monitoring the gamma boundary, and motioned him forward with his fingers.

The man inched his arm forward with the counter's wand. The crackling sound remained unchanged in its intensity. He inched forward, generating a louder, denser crackle. "The boundary has moved," he said in surprise.

Jeremy took a deep breath. Taking tentative steps, he reached for the door handle. The silence behind him highlighted the tension of the moment. Beyond the door, the dark cavern loomed in all its mysteriousness. Somewhere in that darkness lay Bede and Bridget, his two loves—helpless, perhaps dead. Between Jeremy and that darkness stood an EM field and a wall of radiation. If the tables were turned, if he lay there in the darkness in need of help, Bridget would not hesitate. She loved him that much. But it wasn't just love. Love is much weaker than fear, especially the fear of death. It was hope. She saw in every moment a spectrum of possibilities and chose hope. Hope was stronger than fear. Love was irrelevant now. Hope was everything. He opened the door and walked through the glass wall, out to the landing.

"Bridget," he said softly, "I'm coming for you. We're going to help you, honey. But you have to help us." The darkness all around him was punctuated by large sparks. A current rattled him, leaving a metallic taste in his mouth, but there was no pain. He felt it again and again. With each wave, his muscles relaxed involuntarily—but still he felt no pain.

"Bridget, please," he pleaded into the darkness. The waves subsided, though, leaving him in a weakened state.

His foot scraped the floor as he tapped it forward. A few more forward movements, tapping as he progressed, and his foot hit something. It was Bede.

He crouched and felt the body of his brother. There was no way to tell if he was alive, but his radiation suit was still intact. A very good sign, and a little bizarre, given the circumstances. Bridget couldn't be far off. Groping in the darkness on all fours, he reached over Bede's body until he felt the body of his wife. He removed his gloves and tossed them to the side.

"Honey!" He crawled around Bede to her. "Honey, I'm here." He touched her chest and felt his fingers depress into flesh. He pulled back immediately.

Burns!

She moaned very softly. Jeremy gasped, hoping his mind wasn't mistaking the howling gusts for her voice. "You're alive! You're alive, aren't you?" He knelt in front of her. "Honey, I don't know if you have anything to do with this field, but we can't help you as long as it's active. Can you remove it?"

The whistles of the wind currents deep in the cavern responded, but he heard nothing from her. It was hard to hear in the cavern, but with his ear to her face, he heard her rapid breaths.

He rushed back to the doorway and took in the wide-eyed stares. "I don't know what condition Bede's in. He's in his radiation suit still. Bridget has burns, second and third degree. Get a hose out here for preliminary decontamination. We'll need to intubate and get in an intraosseous line... supplemental oxygen."

They all stood rooted to the ground.

"Check the EM field. Check the radiation," he called out. "We have to move quickly."

"Nothing. It's gone," the man with the Geiger counter said as he walked up to the glass wall.

A woman stepped up with an EMF scanner, holding it out until she got to Jeremy. She exhaled loudly and pushed it beyond the boundary of the door. "We're clear! How is that possible?"

As though guided by an unseen hand, in that moment everyone rushed toward a task.

"Can you get her up to the infirmary?" Kate asked. "I'll go notify them now."

Jeremy nodded. "Tell them second and third-degree burns and acute radiation exposure—radiation source unknown."

Kate turned and disappeared into the crowd.

A minute later, a man ran toward them with a long hose with which they sprayed both Bede and Bridget from a distance. After decontamination, a medical crew descended on both to get them stabilized.

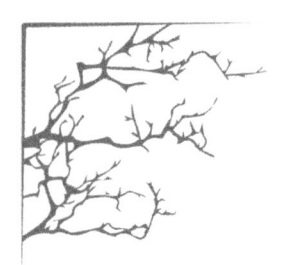

Chapter 12

JEREMY STRAINED TO heave his side of the stretcher; he had refused to let anyone else take the lead. Two people held up the other end and two others had tried to support the weight on the sides, but there wasn't enough room for them all to go up the stairs. Jeremy's solo efforts on his end did not slow the team, though—he made sure of that by summoning every ounce of energy he could muster. The climb went faster than he'd expected. They'd only had to go up one flight to get the elevator to the second floor.

As the elevator doors opened to the second floor, brothers and sisters of the Order rushed to aid them. They took over the stretcher and ran it down to the infirmary, with Jeremy in tow. Once expertly transferred to the medical bed, Bridget became the focus of medical attention. Jeremy watched, helpless.

Brother Juan, a Brother of the Order, tugged gently at his shoulder. "Mr. Blade, I'll be honest with you. It'll be a miracle if she makes it. Besides the radiation exposure, we're looking at full-body third-degree burns." His empathy was as authentic as his firmness about Bridget's prognosis.

Jeremy, agitated, looked around. "Morphine?"

"We can't. Blood pressure is too low."

"Bridget's pain would be intolerable." Jeremy stretched the skin on his temples. "We can't let her wake up."

"You did excellent work getting that line into her bone marrow, but it's the only one we have. My priority is to stave off infection and dehydration. Then we can evaluate for pain treatment. Okay?" He laid a sympathetic hand on Jeremy's shoulder. "We'll be aggressive with the pain control."

Both men turned abruptly toward the entryway as a rush of people rolled Bede into the infirmary. Jeremy's heart skipped at the sight of his brother. There was no way to guess his condition since he was still in the radiation suit.

"Quick, get him into the other room," Brother Juan called out to the group and pulled away from Jeremy to attend to Bede. "Stay here with your wife. If she wakes up, she'll need to see a friendly face."

Jeremy, desperate to see Bede, began to follow the Brother, but stopped. It was true. His primary obligation was to his wife. He turned back, torn, and watched the team work on her.

"BEDE'S GOING TO BE fine. No burns, from what I gathered," Kate said, joining Jeremy and the small crowd of helpers that had gathered around to witness the outcome of Bridget's treatment.

Jeremy exhaled. "Thank you," he whispered gratefully.

Kate left him and wandered around the infirmary, taking pictures. The room was large and generic, bland white walls and a large window with a partial view of the rear of the monastery.

"What are they doing?" Kate asked, pointing at Bridget.

"They're assessing the surface area of the burns," Jeremy replied. "They need the percentage to calculate how much fluid to push in the next twenty-four hours."

"Is she going to make it? Her skin is burnt off all round," Kate said.

"Why stop now, Bridget?" Jeremy responded under his breath, transfixed on the scene unfolding in front of him. He turned to Kate. "The second-degree burns will likely heal. The third-degree burns will need skin grafts. But the burns covered a ninety-percent area. She doesn't have enough skin to graft—but the burns may be the least of our problems. The radiation is more troubling."

"How so?"

"Dr. Jeremy Blade?" A woman behind him tapped his back. "Mabelle Fanetta. I'm... assisting the Interior Ministry in investigating this incident. May we have a word? The sisters were kind enough to give us a room to meet in. I promise this will be quick." Behind her was a tall, chiseled man with thick angry eyebrows, who seemed to regard the whole scene with suspicion.

"Shall we?" Jeremy stretched out his arm, palms up.

They walked into an adjoining room with a few chairs, and Mabelle arranged them. Kate followed them in.

"Madame," Mabelle said to Kate. "This interview is with Dr. Blade. Will you step outside, please?"

"She stays," Jeremy said.

"This is not a matter for the press. She must—"

"She's family... she's my sister." Jeremy maintained his firm gaze.

"We're step-siblings... different parents," Kate picked up the ridiculous ruse.

"Dr. Blade. This is not a game," Mabelle looked back and forth at Jeremy and Kate, whose complexions were many shades apart.

"My wife is dying. You think this is a game for me? Kate stays."

Mabelle looked at her companion and nodded, her face scrunched in obvious displeasure. "A high level of radiation was released about an hour ago. You've identified the radiation as isotropic. It radiated from a single source outward in all directions. We have confirmed that. What, in your opinion, was the source of this radiation event?"

"I don't know."

"Dr. Blade, we have reports that in the rescue of your wife, you walked into—"

"Are these corroborated reports? Do you have any evidence for any of the claims? Are you making a charge?"

"No," she said. "This is an investigation. Thousands of people are dead and injured on our soil. We need to know why, and whether we are still at risk."

"I can't help you." Jeremy's words tumbled out as soon as she was done speaking.

"Your wife was alone in the cavern area just before the emissions. Our scientists have pinpointed her precise location as the epicenter of—"

"Bridget has nothing to do with this," Jeremy shot back. "Are we done? I need to see my wife."

"Dr. Blade, I can hold you in custody—"

The door flung open, and in walked a bearded man in green military fatigues. He wore a black beret and a long braid down his back. "Colonel Tasmi Singh, United States Military Attaché." He handed a badge to Mabelle and gave her a moment to inspect it. He received the badge back and observed both French officials.

"Colonel Singh," Mabelle pointed to the door, at two figures partially covered by the doorway, "who are these men?"

"Gentlemen," Colonel Singh called.

The men, in long jackets, walked in and removed the jackets, revealing military fatigues and automatic rifles.

The man behind Mabelle gasped and reached into his suit.

Tasmi held up his hand. "There's no need for that. These are United States Marines, here to protect United States citizens."

"Colonel, you cannot have U.S. Marines operating outside of authorized zones." Mabelle's loud voice filled the room. "This is an outrage."

"Madame. Do you have an Evidence Request? Or are you charging these citizens with a crime?"

"I am merely conducting an investigation."

"Dr. Blade, Ms. Selz, you may leave. Any inquiries must be directed to Counsel at the American embassy. Bridget Blade, Jeremy Blade, and

Kate Selz will not be contacted or addressed directly. Madame, let me assure you, I may be here talking to you face-to-face, but let me be clear. We are not at the same level. You would do well to kick this matter up to someone well above your pay grade."

Mabelle glared at Colonel Singh and stormed out of the room with her companion.

"Gentlemen," Colonel Singh as he turned to the Marines, "Bridget Blade is not to be removed from that room."

The Marines saluted and jogged out of the room.

"Tasmi!" Jeremy said, grabbing the colonel in a hug. "Just in time. This is Tasmi Singh," he said to Kate. "We were all at The Academy together."

"It's a pleasure, sir," Kate said, following both men, who were walking back to Bridget. "What just happened?"

"I sent word to Tasmi as soon as I could," Jeremy said. "A radiation discharge is always going to be a matter of national interest. We still don't understand what happened, but Bridget appears to be at the center of it. My first thought was to protect her, and Tasmi is as connected and decisive as anyone I know."

"You think they'll accuse her of terrorism?"

"Maybe. But only as a ruse. They, like us, are going to be very interested in the source of the radiation, whether it is somehow naturally occurring, and whether it has to do with Bridget."

They arrived back at Bridget's bedside to find a team of brothers and sisters still working on her.

Tasmi craned his necked to get a good view of Bridget. He closed his eyes and bowed as he muttered a silent prayer. Taking a deep breath, he shook Jeremy's hand. "She'll pull through, my friend. She always has. Call me if you need anything. I must get going."

"I don't think he was authorized to interfere in the Ministry's investigation," Jeremy said softly. "It's a sovereign matter. Imagine if this happened on our soil. I'd say that he's got quite a diplomatic mess to clean up on his end of things." He focused on Bridget. "We have to wait and see how things unfold. She's alive for now, that's all that matters to me."

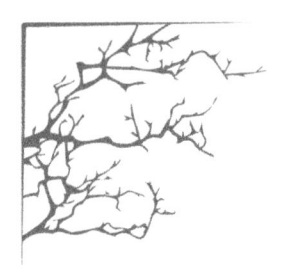

Chapter 13

"EXCUSE ME!" SISTER Kaypore said, pushing two women aside as she dashed out of the elevators toward the infirmary. "We need to clear out the hallway. Who are all these people? What's going on?" she asked a younger sister who'd rushed to meet her.

"It's Dr. Blade," the young Sister said. "I didn't know what to do."

"Is his wife here? What's all that noise?" Sister Kaypore's eyes narrowed in confusion at the apologetic woman running beside her. "I hear Dr. Blade, but who is the other person? Where's his wife?"

She froze as she entered the door of the infirmary. Stationed there were two United States Marines. Her lips parted slightly, but she could not think of anything to say. Her thoughts were disrupted by Jeremy, speaking loudly over another man.

"Excuse me, please." She pushed her way through the small crowd and emerged to find Jeremy standing defiantly in front of a bed. Two Sisters were busy behind him with a patient.

Ignoring the melée, she ran to the bed and screamed in shock at the sight of Bridget. "Theresa! What happened to my baby?"

Everyone stared at her, stunned at her outburst.

She turned to Jeremy. "You said she was downstairs? What happened to her?" Not waiting for a response, and clearly unashamed of being seen in underclothes, she ripped off her bloodied habit and put on a clean one, after which she donned a sterile medical gown and gloves. "Jeremy? What happened?" she said, her voice now much calmer.

"She was out in the cavern, and—"

"She was in the cavern?" Sister Kaypore froze.

"Madame, if you please?" A paramedic stepped forward.

Sister Kaypore looked at Jeremy in confusion. "What is he doing here?"

"Sister," the paramedic said, "He refuses to let us evacuate his wife to a hospital. She's in critical condition."

"This woman is a citizen of the United States. She is my responsibility. She'll remain here," Jeremy responded loudly.

Sister Kaypore pointed back toward the Marines at the entrance. "Jeremy, we can't have armed soldiers in the Monastery. It violates our—"

Jeremy gripped the bed rail. "Bridget is a United States citizen. She is—"

"Jeremy, Jeremy!" she said. "No one's going to harm her. Not with me here."

"Madame," the paramedic said. "We must act—"

"Please leave. Now," Sister Kaypore said. "We have everything we need here to take care of her. She's not going anywhere."

Jeremy looked down at his wife. "There's nothing more we can do for her now. If this is how she is to die, I want her to die here. She would want to die here."

"She's not going to die," Sister Kaypore said, joining the other sisters in applying a salve to Bridget's body. "Give me an update here. Have you run a course of antibiotics? What's in the line here? Fluids? Good. Is her airway clear? What are we doing for pain management?"

"Do you have anesthetics here?" Jeremy asked.

The room became silent.

"You want to induce a coma?" Sister Kaypore asked.

He nodded.

She removed her gloves and held both hands of the paramedic as she thought through her next steps. "Monsieur," she said, "it is okay. We have the facilities here for burn care. She'll need a skin graft. But we have time to decide where to take her. We will make her comfortable here." She urged him backward in the direction of the door. Forcing a smile, she turned to the crowd of about thirty who'd helped with the rescue. "Everything's fine. We'll take care of this."

While some made for the door, the rest lingered, clearly anxious to see the outcome.

A Sister walked up with a covered tray. Sister Kaypore motioned to Jeremy and all three crowded around the intravenous line in Bridget's arm.

"You realize that there's a risk she may never wake up again?" Sister Kaypore whispered. She might as well have shouted. The room became dead silent, in anticipation of Jeremy's response.

"Yes," Jeremy muttered, "but I think she'll make it."

"I do, too. There are no coincidences with her."

The other Sister set about mixing the cocktail and then handed the syringe to Sister Kaypore.

Bridget's breaths were quick and steady, but shallow.

"I should do this," Jeremy offered with resignation, taking in the sight of Bridget lying on the hospital bed. Half of her face revealed red subdermal tissue; the other half was covered in large blisters, rendering her barely recognizable. A large swath of her flayed torso was disconcertingly red, with the skin layers burnt off. Her charred arms and legs lay lifeless on the bed. "She's my wife, and this is my call," he said quietly.

"I understand. But there is no difference in Ryna's eyes between intent and the act. I have no hesitation if you're worried about my conscience. And she is my responsibility." Sister Kaypore fit the syringe into the line. She looked at Jeremy for a moment and then pushed steadily on the syringe, emptying its contents as everyone watched and waited. After a moment, Bridget's breathing slowed. Looking at the monitor, Sister Kaypore said, "She's in a coma. Sister Lysa will let you know of any changes if you want to go and see your brother."

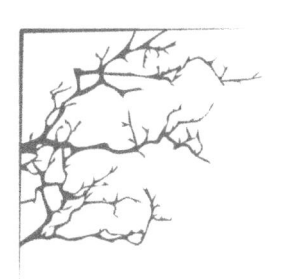

Chapter 14

JEREMY WALKED INTO the adjoining room, dreading what he might see. He breathed a sigh of relief when he saw his brother lying on a bed, his head elevated. He rushed to Bede's side and held his hands gently. "I've never been more frightened than I was walking through this door."

Bede allowed a half-smile as he pointed to his arm and head. "Just mild burns and a concussion, but I've been exposed." He leaned back gingerly on his pillow. "How is Bridget?"

"Not good." Jeremy looked around. Everyone was busy. The Brother helping Bede took his cue, bowed deeply and walked away. "There was a medical helicopter here to evacuate Bridget. I refused to let them. We've induced a coma."

Bede closed his eyes. "What's her diagnosis?"

"Second- and third-degree burns to ninety percent of her body, and she was severely irradiated. I don't know how she's still alive," Jeremy said. "Brother Juan thinks a day at the most. If she was a regular person, I would say less. I don't want her to wake up. Even if she makes it through this, can you imagine the pain?" He got a box of tissues and gave it to his brother, who was struggling to blink back tears.

"I can't imagine life without her," Bede said. "I don't know whether to wish for her to live or die. She was already in so much pain from all the stuff from before. Poison just never leaves her body."

"When you feel up to it, we can set you up to do last rites," Jeremy said.

They sat in silence for a moment. Bede took a sip of water and grimaced at the taste. "Something else bothering you?"

"It's about the equipment. I was trying to help the Sisters with Bridget, and we needed a clear picture of the extent of the radiation event, especially if there was gamma radiation."

Bede's eyes creased in concern. "So what's wrong? We have a few spectrometers. They were downstairs. If you look—"

"All the equipment, all of it, is gone."

Bede pushed and twisted himself upright. "What do you mean, 'gone'? You mean dismantled and stowed for safekeeping?"

"In all the confusion, someone apparently had the presence of mind to carefully pack up *our* equipment, both downstairs and up on the grounds, and get it all out. Apparently, no one noticed because everyone was trying to clean up and get the area ready for the injured."

"Why would anyone do that?" Bede grunted as he repositioned himself.

"Think about it." Jeremy crossed his arms. "Massive radiation discharge, no heat source, no discernible source, period!" Jeremy leaned back like he'd made his point completely clear to his brother. "And then it all disappears, literally without a trace!"

Bede, lost in his thoughts, stared at his brother. "You think the Vatican rep is involved?"

Jeremy nodded.

Bede's face indicated his agreement. "So that makes the helicopter evacuation suspicious—you think it is related to the theft?"

"Someone from the Interior Ministry was here asking questions. They want to know what happened. I've spent the past few hours rounding up every possible resource to help with the crowds up there and then, out of the blue a fully equipped, unaffiliated medevac helicopter arrives specifically for Bridget, shortly after the investigators showed up." Jeremy could barely restrain his irritation. "Someone took a preliminary look at our data and wants more. They know that, based on the radiation, Bridget was at the epicenter of the discharge and she should not be alive. I imagine they want to get their hands on her."

"How have you stopped them?"

Jeremy allowed himself a slight congratulatory smile. "As soon as all this happened and I got my wits about me, I called Tasmi. I knew Bridget would be quite the commodity. It's how I would think."

Bede closed his eyes. "What happened up there, why were resources so scarce? What's going on?"

Jeremy realized now that Bede had no idea of the tragedy outside or of its scale. Of course, there was no way he'd know. "When you get stronger, I can fill you in. I think some radiation from the cavern leaked up to the surface."

"Oh no! Was anyone hurt?"

Jeremy nodded but offered nothing else. Just then, the door swung open.

"Mr. Blade, she's awake! Mrs. Blade's awake!"

Jeremy jumped out of his seat. "That's not possible!" His stomach tightened.

Bede ripped the blood pressure cuff off, pulled out his IV, and swung his legs over the edge of the bed. "I'm coming. Jeremy, help me!"

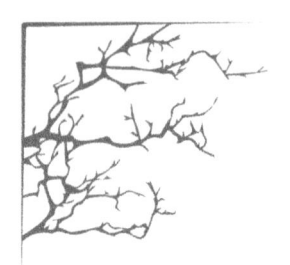

Chapter 15

JEREMY HURRIED HIS weakened brother toward Bridget's full-throated screams.

"Bridget! Bridget! We're here!" Jeremy spoke loudly in her ear, trying to be heard past her screams, which showed no sign of abating. "What happened? She shouldn't be awake," Jeremy said, looking at Sister Kaypore.

"She... she shouldn't..." Sister Kaypore stammered.

Bede cringed visibly with each new bloodcurdling scream. "What's wrong, Sweetheart? Can you tell us? Where's the pain?"

Jeremy gritted his teeth at her screams.

"Bridget, honey, we're here," Bede said.

Her cries reduced to a series of loud sobs.

"Bede, do you remember anything from the cavern? A fall? Anything that can help us?"

"Bits and pieces—she did fall: there were these really bright flashes. When they stopped, Bridget was pure black—spectrum black."

"I've seen this before," Sister Kaypore said. "Did she glow?"

"Yes, from black to a bluish glow," Bede replied.

"She was the source and she reabsorbed it," Sister Kaypore said. "I mean total absorption across the spectrum."

"You mean that she must've absorbed everything on the light spectrum after the initial discharge?" Bede asked. "It's plausible. I have never seen anything so black."

Jeremy held Bridget's bandaged hands. "Bede, she was in control of whatever happened down there. I walked through an EM field with all that radiation and I am fine. In fact, it vanished when I asked her to help us."

"You what?" Bede asked.

"What does your equipment register?" Sister Kaypore asked.

"It's all missing," Jeremy said. "But some of the guys have done continual sweeps with their equipment. Nothing. There's no residual radiation."

"So there was a burst of radiation," Bede said. "It didn't dissipate. It didn't register beyond a certain radius, and then it disappeared. You're suggesting it contracted back to its source? Her? If so, she should be burning, but that isn't the case."

"Actually, Padre, I've had to send for different thermometers," Sister Kaypore said. "Her outer body feels normal, but her internal temperature is off the charts. Either all our thermometers are defective or they don't go high enough."

Bridget's cries picked back up, and soon her screams filled the room again.

Jeremy's tight grip on the railing stiffened with each torturous cry.

"If you're right, then she would be burning internally." Bede inhaled. "I hope to God we're wrong. I can't even imagine waking to that kind of pain."

"Her eyes are open!" Jeremy pointed.

Bede waved his hand in front of her face. "I don't think she can see anything. Oh, Bridget, hang in there. We love you."

"Jeremy! Jeremy! Where's Jeremy?" Each cry of his name was a desperate plea.

"Here, honey! I'm here, honey. I'm here!"

"Help me! Please!" Her screams changed to loud moans, each ending with a sob, over and over. Her body trembled violently as though reacting to recurring waves of pain.

"Can't we give her anything?" Bede asked.

Sister Kaypore shook her head. "We've given everything we can. She shouldn't be awake." She looked at Jeremy with eyes full of despair. "Let's push some more morphine," she said.

Bede leaned over on the other side of the bed and stroked Bridget's head. "We love you. We're here." He repeated this over and over. Her cries gradually reduced to persistent, low, guttural moans. Her neck strained in a slight arch and her hollow, unblinking eyes were fixed on the ceiling.

"Bede! Bede! Help me!" She started up again.

"I'm here, Bridget. I'm here," he replied as he gently stroked her cheek. Eventually, the moaning reduced to a series of whimpers. "She's fighting." His voice quivered as he looked up at Jeremy and Sister Kaypore. "It's all she can do or she'll go mad!"

A bloodcurdling scream emerged from her lips, startling everyone. Loud static sounded from the direction of a dresser a few meters away.

"That's the Geiger counter!" Sister Kaypore said. "She's emitting radiation."

"Everyone out!" Bede's shout rang out, followed by a rush of people pulling gurneys with patients and equipment out, although some members of the Order remained.

"Bridget, honey," Jeremy said calmly. "You have to contain it. There are too many people here, and I know you don't want to hurt anyone."

"The radius is fifteen meters, but just stops there," Sister Kaypore said, holding the Geiger counter wand. With careful steps, she traced an arc until she got to the wall. "Isotropic. Quick, Brother Juan, clear a twenty-meter radius on the other side of the wall and all around. I think we're dealing with gamma radiation. God help us."

"Bridget, sweetie," Jeremy spoke softly. "I know it hurts. It burns. I can't imagine what you're going through, somehow your body is unstable and releasing energy and particles. You've never harmed anyone, don't start now. Take it back in, please."

The infirmary was silent except for the crackling of the Geiger counter. A moment later, the static decreased.

Sister Kaypore reached out. "Fourteen feet... thirteen... ten... it's receding. She's reabsorbing it. We're all clear now."

"It hurts! It hurts so much!" Bridget said between cries, and then screamed at the top of her lungs.

A thick blackness enveloped the room and slowly thinned until it receded. In its place, an indigo hue flooded the room, and then slowly transformed back to regular light.

"She must be pulsing," Sister Kaypore said quietly, as though conversing with herself. "The Wave. It must be the Wave."

"What do you mean, Sister?" Jeremy asked with furrowed brow. "Do you know something that can help us?"

"Jeremy, we can't let this go on," Bede said. "She has to release it."

"It's her or everyone else," Jeremy replied. "She would never intentionally hurt anyone. I can't let her live with that guilt."

A shrill beep interrupted them, jarring everyone within earshot. Bridget's desperate cries continued. Everyone rushed to the machine that registered her vital signs. The numbers indicating her temperature raced up until the machine read, "Error."

"Bridget, my sweet baby," Sister Kaypore crooned, holding her hand. "Push it into me. Release it into me! Let me help you! You're the only reason I live."

"No. Bridget, no!" Jeremy spoke loudly and stared at Sister Kaypore, confused by her seeming familiarity with Bridget. "I know her. She would rather live with this pain than destroy you."

"Jeremy?"

"Sister," Jeremy said gently, "I have spent most of my waking hours as an adult with this woman. You have no idea what guilt and emotional pain do to her. She would choose a thousand hells over harming another human. This is her hell, but she has made the choice. All she wants from us is love. That's what we can do to aid her."

"No one should or can endure this much pain," Sister Kaypore said.

"She's doing it," Jeremy said. He'd always felt like no one except him could ever understand Bridget, until now. Sister Kaypore, who'd just met Bridget a couple of hours ago, had a connection with Bridget he couldn't even fathom. How?

"Can we transport her somewhere so she can release it all?" Bede asked, interrupting Jeremy's thoughts.

"No," Jeremy said. "Until we know who took our equipment and who's behind the man who wanted to medevac her, we should keep her here. And let's be honest, there's nowhere that's safe for that amount of radiation. Keep her here. She needs love. All she needs is someone here telling her how much they love her. I promise you, it'll sustain her."

Bridget's cries had become tearful sobs.

"May we attend to her?" A Sister walked up to Sister Kaypore.

Jeremy nodded. "We're exposed already. There's—"

"It's of no consequence to me," the Sister said. "My life is God's to be reaped at her will."

"It's a simple matter of chemistry, isn't it?" Bede said. "She may have pulled through other things, but the molecular bonds can't hold, not through all this."

"Let's think good thoughts," Sister Kaypore whispered. "Like you, I don't see a way. But faith, hope, and love are all choices. Let's make the positive choice." She squeezed both men's hands and joined the young sister who was helping with Bridget.

It had been thirty minutes since all this started. Jeremy looked at his brother, who held Bridget's hand while stroking a little patch of Bridget's remaining hair. Bede, always the pillar of strength, had to be fatigued. Jeremy turned to Sister Kaypore. "Can you have someone bring Bede's bed so that he can lie next to her and hold her hand?"

"Absolutely!" She motioned to Brother Juan, who ran into the adjoining room. In a few moments, Bede's hospital bed was wheeled in and positioned next to Bridget's. They laid Bede on it with a pillow supporting both his and Bridget's arms. Bede fell asleep almost immediately, but Bridget didn't. Her unrelenting cries continued throughout the night.

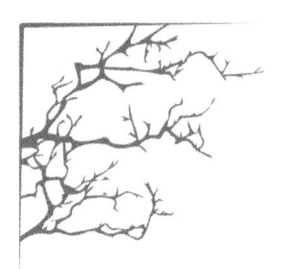

Chapter 16

"HERE. TAKE MY HAND." Kate reached out to help steady Jeremy as he made his way down a boulder. She anchored herself to a low tree branch and guided him until he was down on the ground. She then inched her way down the rock, holding on to the branch until she was close enough to the ground, and jumped off.

Bright flashes illuminated the worn clay clearing as she lifted the camera around her neck and took a few pictures. She bemoaned the shade and the late afternoon light, which would soon give way to dusk. There was very little evidence of the prior day's events here at the cavern.

"I'm always in awe of this place," she said as they approached the large cavern opening, which rose from the ground like a giant mouth stretching out in a frozen yawn. Minimalist carvings adorned the archway entrance, which led down into a wonderland of stalagmites and stalactites.

Jeremy nodded at a few people, mostly tourists, a few pilgrims, and some journalists as they stood at the threshold with blue tape barring entrance. "Down there," he whispered, "deep down is where it all happened. The radiation must have swept up the cave and fanned out. But after that initial wave, nothing. Nothing around is irradiated, not the injured, the sick, the dead, no one who was exposed has any trace of radiation. We measured it, recorded it, saw the effects—we know there was a discharge, but it all just disappeared without a trace. The radius was four miles. Beyond that, no one has reported registering any unusual radiation. That's not a natural phenomenon."

Kate stepped back and took more pictures. "You think it has to do with Bridget?"

"Yes. You saw what happened in the infirmary," he replied.

"Let's go this way," Kate said, pointing to the west of the cavern entrance. She waited for Jeremy to catch up. They climbed past another set of boulders bordering the cavern's entrance and found themselves back in the woods. "You were right. Ryna is being blamed for all this. My editors want a story about the tension between Thysians and Ryneans. There's no shortage of Thysians who want to pile on Ryna. I just can't find anyone high profile enough to represent Ryna. No one wants to be associated with her right now."

"I will," Jeremy said. "Why didn't you ask me?"

"Jeremy," she turned to him. "You've given me so much. Letting me tag along and report whatever I want. I feel insensitive thinking of my story when Bridget lays there dying. Besides, you took a stance on camera before the whole world when I interviewed you earlier."

"It's okay. I would be glad to talk. Anything to get my mind off all this."

She took in a grateful breath of the cool evening air. The grounds and woods, though busy with police, tourists, and many others, were a stark contrast to Bridget's grating cries. They walked in silence until all the busyness had subsided, leaving them alone with the forest and its natural evening rhythms. It would take about thirty minutes to get back to the monastery. As calm as Jeremy was externally, he was clearly distracted and agitated. He needed to get back to Bridget. Kate wanted to get back, too, but Sister Kaypore had assured her that Bridget wouldn't die while they were gone. She had insisted that Kate take Jeremy for a walk, as far away from the monastery as she could manage.

Kate needed background for her story, but she was hesitant. Jeremy, hands in his jacket pockets, stared straight ahead and walked with a mechanical gait. His face, locked in a neutral expression, revealed nothing—neither despair nor hope. She'd seen many photos of him in the past and he'd often had that look, the look of a man searching the horizon in vain.

In the past couple of days, he'd vacillated between warmth and coolness. Sometimes she thought she could feel in him a deep well of love as he stared motionlessly at Bridget. At other times, his gaze turned to stone and Bridget was simply an object of fascination. She'd seen his finger on Bridget with a touch so light, yet flush with so much emotion, as he embraced her with his soul. At other times, the same light touch was that of a man who'd discovered something rare, who couldn't believe his luck. Either way, he was captivated by his wife in ways Kate could not fathom. His vicissitude was more than just a coping mechanism. There seemed to be something in him that had shut off, and she wished she could reach inside and turn it back on. Bridget certainly could use all the love he could give her, and Kate was convinced he had much more to give.

"Tell me about the Establishment, three hundred years ago, when the prophets first revealed Thysia," she said, hoping to draw him back to the present.

"They didn't reveal her. There was nothing to reveal," he answered. "Ryna created the world and has been its god for all of history. The Establishment is simply a moment of human hubris. These 'prophets' rejected Ryna because they didn't like following her practices."

"Specifically, they didn't like her constant demand for sacrifices? So they... introduced Thysia?" Kate asked. "My grandmother loved Ryna," she chuckled, "but warned us to never marry a Rynean. She said Ryna would make us sacrifice our first child." Jeremy didn't respond, but he blinked in a steady pattern as his eyes darted back and forth. "So, you don't think Thysia exists as an independent god?" she asked.

"No, although most of her followers do."

He sighed and stopped to lean on a tree. He closed his eyes and she worried he would nod off, but he opened them after a minute. They were worn and bloodshot, framed by worry lines that creased his forehead. She wanted to hug him and reassure him, but not now. She was working.

"The founding prophets rejected Ryna, and people flocked to them," Jeremy continued. "They offered a sanitized version of Ryna. It was in the second generation of the movement that the founding priests emerged. They came up with the name *Thysia*. It was the priests who proposed the idea that Thysia was another god to whom Ryna was subject. Thysia means 'sacrifice,' and they said that Thysia would more readily sacrifice herself for the people than demand that her people sacrifice themselves for her. It's why there is such confusion and tension between the Thysian priests and the Thysian people. Ironically, it's the Thysian priesthood that's been the moderating force. They've given Ryneans the right to remain faithful to Ryna."

"Would they shut you all down now?" Kate asked.

"No. To discredit Ryna, would ultimately be to discredit Thysia. The Vatican and the priesthood know that. It's why they tolerate us."

"So, give me a quote. Something to the effect that Ryna should not be blamed for this," she said.

"The more I think about it, the less sure I am." His gaze wandered up toward the tree tops. "This is precisely what Ryna does—reaps the souls of her faithful. It usually means she's owed something, or she's given something."

"At least four thousand dead or injured, by early estimates. What could she possibly give that's worth that?" Kate asked. He shook his head. "No wonder no one would talk to me," she chuckled. "I can't print that."

She watched him breathe heavily. "Sit down with me," she said as she helped him down to the base of a tree. She held his left hand in both of hers. "I wish I could do something for you. You haven't slept in two days."

"I don't know what to do," he said as his voice cracked. His eyes welled up and a solitary tear trailed down his cheek. She wanted to wipe it, but he had her hand in a tight clasp. "I don't know what to do. I want to do what Bridget would want. Everyone thinks I know what she would want. I know she would want to die here at the monastery. But every moment she's alive in agony, I curse myself for not letting them take her to the hospital. You have to understand, she would hate to die in a hospital when the Monastery of Light was so close. I feel horrible for being so angry at her these past few days. How was I supposed to know this would happen?"

She watched him bend his head and sob quietly, his head tilted away from her. She leaned over and rested her head on his shoulder to let him know he was not alone. Her interview would have to wait. They remained sitting for several minutes.

"Are you ready to go?" she asked quietly. They'd been gone an hour, and it was time to get back. It was early twilight, and the sky was beginning to darken ever so slightly. He nodded and let her help him up. "I don't understand everything you're feeling, but you are a wonderful husband and I think Bridget's lucky to have you."

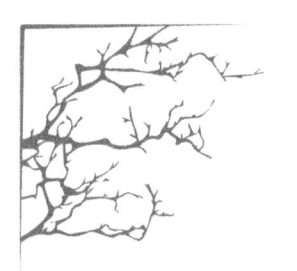

Chapter 17

KATE SAT ON THE FLOOR outside the infirmary, her head buried in her knees and her hands over her ears. Bridget's jarring screams pierced the hallways so wrenchingly that all the other patients had to be moved off the floor.

"How can I help you, Bridget?" she whispered to herself. "Tell me."

Bridget's screams were all reactive. She never once asked the team to stop. The necrotic tissue from her third-degree burns needed to be cut out to prevent infection. After Jeremy's minor meltdown earlier he'd decided, with Sister Kaypore's blessing, to keep her at the monastery. Sister Kaypore, Jeremy and Bede, with the help of other Brothers and Sisters, decided to proceed with the operation. It had taken a lot of work to convert the infirmary into a sterile room. Kate had been asked to run large white sheets over and over again through the washer and dryer. The sheets were used to cover the entire room.

Kate wished she could see what was going on in there. There was no doubt that the people who loved Bridget most were in there and would offer as much care as necessary. But *she* needed to give Bridget a hug and tell her everything would be fine. What a brave soul. The pain meds no longer seemed to work, and the only relief Bridget ever got was when she passed out in exhaustion and pain.

The shrill screams had ended after an hour and been replaced by loud sobs. The door swung open, and out came a determined Jeremy, looking uncharacteristically informal—a loose t-shirt and loose pants. Bede followed almost immediately.

"What's going on?" Kate jumped up and followed them toward the elevator. Jeremy was on the phone with someone. Kate couldn't figure out what was happening from the bits of conversation she could hear.

Jeremy held the elevator door open until she got in.

"Bede?" she asked.

"We may have... a donor possibility," he responded. His eyes, directed downward, refused to meet hers. Bede was reserved but direct. He only avoided gazes when he felt bad about something. What was Jeremy up to?

"Jeremy?" she asked as he clicked off the phone.

The elevator opened up to the cavern floor and both men ran out through the hallway. Jeremy motioned to her and she ran with them. They stopped at a bed at the end of the brightly lit hallway, where a woman stood over a body.

"Thank you, Jeana. What do we have here?" Jeremy asked.

"Time of death was less than twenty minutes ago. Would she work?" Jeana responded.

Bede stepped back and looked the other way, toward the Brothers, who were scrubbing the walls diligently in an attempt to remove the vestiges of the past few days. Bede clearly wanted no part of this decision.

"She's perfect," Jeremy said. "The complexion is similar. Can we get her washed and prepped?"

"Jeremy?" Kate looked up at him. "You want to use her skin on Bridget? That's disgusting."

"It's standard," he said, walking around the body and inspecting it. "Bridget doesn't have enough good skin for a proper graft. Every minute without her skin, she's losing moisture and is at an increased risk of infection."

"Who is this woman? I'm assuming she consented to this."

Kate received no answer.

"This is not right. She never gave consent."

"She's dead. That would be hard," Jeremy said.

"Jeremy!" Kate snapped.

"I don't mean to be flippant—"

Kate turned to Jeana, who'd been watching the exchange wide-eyed. She had her hands on the gurney, as though ready to proceed with Jeremy's instructions.

"Did you withhold life-saving treatment from this woman?" Kate asked.

Jeana's lip twitched.

"Yes," Jeremy said. "I gave instructions that once a suitable candidate was identified, if death seemed inevitable, then let the natural process play out."

"I can't believe you would do this."

Jeremy waved Jeana away. "You've seen what I've seen in the past couple of days. No human being should be able to survive or do what Bridget's done. This is not just surviving a snake bite, bacterial infection, or wild mushrooms. Bridget generated and controlled an electromagnetic field. She emitted ionizing radiation! Yes. She is far more important to the world than you or I or this dead person here."

"Is that what Bridget is to you? A scientific specimen?"

Jeremy glared at Kate but didn't respond.

"I'm sorry. I didn't mean that," she said. "I know you love her and care for her more than I can ever know. But..." She didn't know what else to say.

"What has happened is a fact. There either is a science to it, or there isn't. If there is, what we learn from Bridget could save billions of people. I see this as a win-win. I possibly get my wife back and the world learns something."

"This is not the way we advance," Kate said. "We have to be ethical about what we do. Otherwise, we lose sense of why we're helping each other in the first place."

"Bridget is enough of a 'why' for me."

"Jeremy. You can't speak for me, for this woman, much less for all of humanity. You can only give what is yours. Don't make that decision for others."

Both turned as Bede cleared his throat. She'd forgotten he was there.

"We should proceed," he said quietly.

"Bede, you're a priest. Don't you have a problem with all this?"

Bede took a deep breath and walked toward Jeremy. "Kate, you don't understand my brother. He will flay himself for Bridget—"

"Then let him do it!"

Bede forced Jeremy to turn and pulled up his shirt.

Kate gasped, seeing a large dressing covering an area of Jeremy's back. The dressing was soaked with patches of blood. "Jeremy, what did you do?"

"You are not the first to have this discussion with him. There was no hesitation. It was him or her," Bede said, pointing at the cadaver.

"Who did this?" Kate asked feeling around his back. "Are you in pain?"

Neither man responded, but Bede glared at the woman who'd been waiting by the cadaver. Kate figured she was must have been the one to agree to harvest his skin.

"I don't know if this is love, narcissism, or plain ol' folly." She leaned on Jeremy's chest and gave him a soft hug. The walls were still wet from the scrubbing, but they seemed clean. What Jeremy was about to do didn't. Backing up against the wall, she sat and stared at the trio as they pulled the gurney away from her, down the corridor, and into the elevator.

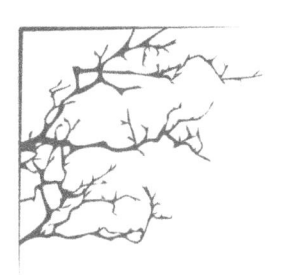

Chapter 18

BRIDGET'S SITUATION had now escalated into an international affair. The French government had attempted to sequester her, demanding to take her immediately into custody because of her possible role in the unexplained release of intense radiation which had resulted in the injuries and deaths of thousands of pilgrims. Jeremy, with the aid of U.S. Marines, had prevented the French government from gaining physical custody of his wife. As a result, a meeting had been called to decide who had a legitimate legal claim to Bridget's body.

Jeremy, frazzled and frayed, struggled to remain alert. He had been awake for three days straight, most of that time spent listening to Bridget enduring the worst pain imaginable. She was being burned alive by radiation she'd inexplicably absorbed into her body. Compared to that, none of this seemed important.

As much as he loved matching wits at meetings like this, he was in no condition to represent Bridget's best interests—it was a task best left to others. He was only here to observe the exchange. He took a sip of his tea and awkwardly set it down, almost tipping the saucer over.

"You okay, my friend?" Colonel Tasmi Singh asked.

Jeremy grunted in his direction and took a deep breath. He stared at his clasped hands and dozed off for a moment, snapping back at the sound of Bridget's name. He looked to his right; it was the French official. Jeremy couldn't remember which agency she represented, but at this point it didn't matter. It was enough to note that she represented the French government, which was cooperating with the Vatican, even though they made a show of being independent of each other.

"We have lodged our protest. We will not accept active United States Marines on our soil—"

"Protecting an American citizen." Jeremy, alert now, interrupted the French official. She glared at him, eyes flashing with malice. He returned the glare, but he was too tired to match her intensity. His gaze shifted outward to the beautiful skyline, and then out to the hills, in the direction of the Monastery of Light. Bridget would be in agony, as she'd been the past few days. Thankfully, the Brothers and Sisters had been generous with their time and care for Bridget. Bede was relatively well, given his degree of radiation exposure. He had responded well to treatment, but it was only a matter of time before his body would succumb to all that radiation.

"The Vatican wishes, again, to emphasize that the Monastery of Light is sovereign territory, an extension of the Vatican's consulate. We have a claim to everything in that monastery. Further, the disposal of any and all property is the prerogative of the Vatican."

Jeremy's tired eyes lingered on the genial-looking priest with wire-rimmed glasses. He seemed uncomfortable in this setting, and Jeremy wondered why he was here. It was probably because he was a naturally sympathetic figure, and it would be difficult to get angry at him. After all, the claim to sovereignty was such a ridiculous one that anyone who would make that claim with a straight face was admirable, and yet this man pulled it off. He actually appeared to believe his claim. On the other hand, Jeremy simmered because no one would acknowledge his missing equipment, even though someone in this room, most likely the priest, knew where it was and who was examining its data.

The American ambassador to his left snickered. "Padre, you are surely not going to continue to insist that an archaic eighteenth-century rule should govern our deliberations here?" He looked around. "Look, we've been going around and around on this issue for days. Let's put our cards on the table, shall we? We are all very interested in Bridget Blade as a specimen." Removing his glasses, he wiped them as he leaned sideways into Jeremy. "Jeremy, our thoughts and prayers are with you in this very difficult time. No one here wishes to diminish your beautiful and wonderful wife in any way." He squeezed Jeremy's hand. "She's going to die soon. We will perform an autopsy, and the results will be shared with all interests here."

"Well, sir," the French official responded quickly, "this event happened on French soil. It is a matter of French sovereignty. People died. We're affected. Besides, let's address the obvious and pressing question. Where did that radiation come from—and where did it go? Bridget Blade's body must remain in French custody as we continue this very *active* investigation," she proclaimed with emphasis, scanning the room. "Any other conclusion or result will be a violation of our national sovereignty."

"A squad of your finest domestic forces surrounding the monastery belies your diplomatic charm," the American ambassador spoke. His gestures were minimal, in contrast to his earlier agitation.

Mr. Wei, the Chinese ambassador, cleared his throat. He'd said very little in the past hour. "Well, um, obviously, the Chinese have no territorial claims here." They all chuckled. He continued, "But I support my colleague, my American friend. Citizenship claims must take priority over territorial sovereignty claims. Bridget Blade is a Chinese citizen…" The room erupted in discussion but soon calmed down. "Dr. Blade's mother is Chinese. Bridget Blade grew up in China. She was sent to The Academy from China as a Chinese contribution to The Academy." His index finger tapped the wooden table as he spoke.

"Mr. Wei," the American ambassador said loudly, "I grant you that she does have dual citizenship. But, to be clear, her father is American, she identifies as American, and she has traveled widely as an American."

"Yes, sir, but let's face it, her father is African American. He moved to China because he is a second-class citizen in your country. He could not vote or even drink water from the same water fountain as you. He would, even now, be forced to ride at the back of the bus." He let his words settle and then continued. "She was born and raised in China. We discovered her. We discovered her mind. We sent her to The Academy, even when we could have tried to nurture her talent in our own country, exclusively for our benefit. I think we have a stronger citizenship and moral claim here. The government of the People's Republic of China demands the corpse of Bridget Blade."

Silence filled the room. Jeremy understood how the game was played. In these situations, everyone knew the most likely outcome, which in this case was that the U.S. would get its way, even though the French had primacy here. The key for the other players was to utilize whatever leverage one had to negotiate the best deal. Talking and negotiating diplomatically never hurt. Outbursts and anger hardly ever helped. Thus, against his instincts, Jeremy decided it was time to depart and leave Tasmi and the ambassador to represent his interests, which he had no doubt they would do.

Jeremy cleared his throat and took a deep breath. "Well, this is a mess, isn't it? I have to leave. I hope, as you discuss this situation, that you all remember that you are talking about a human being. That sweet woman—" he took a couple of breaths and stared through the window. "—and she is a very sweet woman—is my wife. I'm a scientist and you all know, as much as anyone else, I am curious about everything about this. But she's my wife first and foremost. If you want to make a decision about her, come and listen to her moan in pain, in agony, for hours and hours, maybe that'll give you some perspective."

He took one last sip of his tea. He stood and took a deep bow, signaling his desire to leave. Everyone stood up and bowed in return. As he walked away, he heard the chairs slowly return to their positions as the negotiators sat down. No one spoke until he was out of earshot.

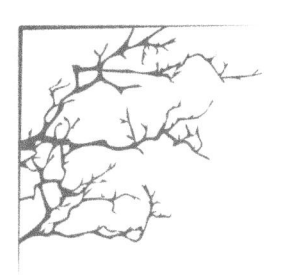

Chapter 19

BRIDGET AWAKENED TO a sound, but tried to will herself back into a sleep state, hoping for respite from exhausting and unrelenting pain. She could see nothing more than fuzzy blobs of light, and, she couldn't smell anything but an acrid and fetid odor. Fiery waves radiated through her as though from a furnace trapped within her, creating a deep, scalding sensation.

However, beyond the physical sensations, she buckled under an unyielding weight, and that was the real terror—to find herself the object of the inevitable march of death. But if death was the irresistible force backing her off the cliff, she sensed no edge behind her. Each moment stretched out interminably as she waited in fear for the end to come, but death pushed and pushed, and yet nothing.

"Who's there?" She called out in a raspy voice, followed by a whimper.

"Hi, honey." Sister Kaypore's voice clashed with her approaching footsteps. "It's Sister Kaypore. You wouldn't remember me. How are you?"

"She won't snap the cord—send me over." Bridget's whisper was hoarse.

"I don't understand, honey," Sister Kaypore responded.

"I want to die, Sister. Why won't She let me die?" She felt herself yield to the kind presence next to her.

"Her ways are mysterious, Bridget. She loves you! We all love you very much!" Sr. Kaypore touched Bridget's fingers lightly.

"Where's Jeremy?" Bridget asked. Every movement seemed to stretch a nerve, causing raw pain.

"He's been here non-stop. There was a meeting regarding your... care... and he had to be there." She paused, stroking Bridget's bandaged arm. "Bede's not available right now. He's... He'll be back soon."

"There's someone else here," Bridget said. She moaned.

"Yes, it's... I'm Kate Selz. We met... downstairs."

Bridget heard a set of quiet footsteps approach. "Kate," she said. The crushing weight had lifted and there was nothing holding her any longer. She could fly away to Ryna's arms if she wanted. The struggle was no longer resisting a weight, her fight was now to remain grounded, to keep from floating off. "Kate... help my husband?" Speaking was enervating. She was losing strength and no longer replenishing it. "It can't be long now? I can't hold on anymore."

Neither Kate, nor Sister Kaypore said anything. In the relative darkness, they listened to Bridget's groans and offered words of comfort.

"She's getting less oxygen," Sister Kaypore whispered, pointing to a monitor.

"Listen," Kate said, holding the Sister's arm. "She's quiet."

Bridget's breathing was now fast and labored, but there were no groans.

"Can you take me outside?" Bridget's voice sounded like she was straining under a very heavy weight. "Please." She took in a few breaths. "Let me touch the earth."

"Bridget, Jeremy and Bede are not here. You have to hold on. They'll be back soon," Kate replied.

"Please, let me touch the earth." Bridget's plea ended in a sob. She whimpered and became quiet again.

"What is she talking about?" Kate whispered to Sister Kaypore.

"If she dies having touched the earth, her soul will find its way to Ryna faster," Sister Kaypore said.

"Can you arrange this?" Kate asked, "for her to touch the earth? It's the least we can do."

Sister Kaypore stared at Bridget. Her lips moved as though she were uttering a silent prayer. She seemed uncharacteristically confused.

"Sister?"

"Stay here with her," Sister Kaypore said. "I'll arrange this."

Kate watched the sister run out of the infirmary. She continued to stroke the remaining patch of Bridget's hair—the only exposed part of her body anyone had been allowed to touch, other than her hand.

"Can you sing to me, please?" Bridget squeaked.

She held Bridget's coarse hand delicately. Something had changed. The frenzy of the past few days had evaporated, leaving peace and quietude in its wake. The few Rynean songs her grandmother had taught her were upbeat and unsuited to the moment. Thysian hymns seemed a better fit. Hoping no one would take offense, here in the seat of Ryna, she took a deep breath, closed her eyes, and began to sing. The deep, rhythmic clangs of the tower bell rang overhead, sweeping Kate into a place of transcendent ecstasy, a place beyond voice, dance, touch, or sight.

A rush of footsteps sounded down the corridor but halted at the doorway. Kate was now conscious of the sound of her song filling the room as she held Bridget's hand more tightly. Muted footsteps and hushed activity spread all around her. She felt a soft kiss on her cheek and opened her eyes to Sister Kaypore's sweet smile. If they were offended by a Thysian hymn, they showed no indication of it. In fact, they seemed to encourage it with their smiles and humming. A group of Brothers and Sisters, careful not to disturb Kate, unwrapped and cut all Bridget's bandages. Using the bedsheet, they moved Bridget off the bed into a reclining chair. Bridget's breathing rate increased in response to the activity, but she made no sound.

Sister Kaypore kissed the pale Bridget, who now seemed to have withdrawn into herself. If she was aware of anything or anyone, it was no longer evident. Her labored, rapid breaths rattled in her chest, punctuated by moments when she stopped breathing altogether.

"Bridget, honey, Jeremy and Bede are on their way," Sister Kaypore said softly in Bridget's ear. She knelt next to Bridget. "Please hang on till they arrive. I don't understand this moment, why this is happening. But I have learned faith these past thirty-odd years. If this is your moment, then it is, and I accept it. My life's work has not been in vain. Thirty-five years ago, I would not have been able to accept a conclusion like this—it was contrary to what I knew to be true. But meeting you and your people was the best thing that has ever happened to me. Maybe that's how I will save my people—by teaching them the faith of your people. Maybe that was the way all along. I love you, my sweet girl. I will always love you."

The elevator ride seemed shorter than usual. When the door opened in the main lobby, a path opened through the crowd of Brothers and Sisters who'd come to escort Bridget outside in her last moments. Kate gasped as the large wooden doors opened, spilling glorious sunlight into the lobby. Bridget's hand was weak and fragile in hers. The bubbly person she'd met a few days ago was now a distant memory. But here, this fragile person, this brittle shell, was on the verge of sprouting into a vibrant reality beyond the world of shadow. Kate now understood the privilege of being reaped by Ryna, the moment of true realization that we are nothing and She is everything, when we give up all that we are to be all that She is. The Thysians had it wrong. God can't sacrifice for us. All that God is must be earned by our full sacrifice. How else are we to show that we are worthy of the divine nature?

"Thank you, Lord," Sister Kaypore whispered loudly, bring her hand to her heart. "Thank you for this euthanasia—this beautiful death."

Kate smiled at the Sister and her prayer. Sister Kaypore pushed Bridget outward to the pavilion which, days before, had been the site of an unimaginable tragedy. Thousands had died. Now the grounds beyond were filled with hundreds of memorials. Each small pile of flowers, notes, rocks, and stuffed animals celebrated lives Ryna had taken.

Bridget, still and peaceful, was covered in a short white sheet tucked into the sides of the reclining chair. Her uncovered arms and feet revealed large patchworks of grafted pale brown skin.

Sister Kaypore laid her hand on Kate's shoulder. "I'll take her to the woods, just to the tree line, and there I'll let her touch the earth."

Kate's eyes watered as she looked at Bridget. "Can I do this? It would mean so much to me."

"Yes, of course," Sister Kaypore said. She took a deep breath. "Pick up a handful of earth and place it in her hand so that she can hold it. Hold her hand if necessary. Then pray. Call to Ryna." She paused. "Rhee-nay!" She spoke quietly. "That's the proper way to address her. Call to her and say 'Ryna, the golden cord is broken. The flower of the earth is returned to thee.' Okay?"

Kate nodded eagerly, repeating the verse silently.

Sister Kaypore kissed Kate on the forehead, and they all watched as Kate pushed the chair to the woods several hundred yards away.

Kate turned around to see everyone. They all looked particularly distant and small in contrast to the looming trees. After fighting to push the chair through the soft soil until she was well past the tree line, she sat down in front of Bridget, whose face was now losing its color. Kate gathered up a handful of dirt; it was filled with roots, a little grass, and a few bugs. It didn't matter. The soil was dark, rich, and organic—seemingly appropriate for the moment.

"Bridget, I don't know if you can hear me." She knelt next to Bridget and leaned back on her heels. "I grew up in a Thysian household. It's never meant much to me. I knew of Ryneans and, quite frankly, I always thought you all were very strange, with your customs, your superstitions, your love of raw nature." She paused. "But here I am, sharing this beautiful moment with you. Believing this moment with you." She looked around and up toward the tops of the trees. "It feels like a temple here," she whispered.

She took Bridget's limp right hand, carefully turned the dirt over into it, and held it shut. She held Bridget's left hand, closed her eyes, took a deep breath, and recited the verse:

"Ryna, the golden cord is broken. The flower of the earth is returned to thee."

She stilled herself to honor the moment.

"Ryna, if you can hear me, please take this beautiful soul into your care."

She opened her eyes, unsure of what to do next. There was no hurry now. She wiped a tear at the corner of her eye. "I just wanted to tell you that my reports from here have done wonders for my career. Jeremy, Bede, and Sister have been so kind. I've had access to everything. I can now take any assignment or job I want. I can go back to the States or remain in Europe. It's exciting." She paused to listen to Bridget's halting, weak breaths. "You told me that I was not invisible... I believed you... I believe you. Thank you so much. Your words meant more than you could ever know." She studied Bridget's face. "You are the most beautiful woman I have ever seen."

She rubbed Bridget's exposed forearm. "I'm sorry that neither Bede nor Jeremy can be here. I know they'll be devastated. But I promise you, I'll help them through this. I suppose we'll help each other."

She thought she felt a very slight squeeze. Her heart skipped. *She can hear me!* "This may be strange, but I love you, Bridget." She removed her necklace. "This," looking at the thin golden bird on the necklace, "was given to me by my grandmother. She was Rynean, but converted to Thysia. She always said they were the same." She shrugged. "She gave this to me just before she died." Her voice cracked. "I want to you to have it. Tell Mama that I love her when you see her. You will see her. She, too, was a flower of the earth. Like you, she gave everyone so much to believe in." She wiped her eyes.

An unusual sound, like the low distant horn of a faraway ship, reverberated through the woods. She let go of Bridget's hand and slowly stood. Another sound, a rustling from her right, caught her attention. Losing her balance momentarily, she turned in alarm as the movement traced a semi-circle around them. Lightheaded with fear and thoroughly spooked, she started back toward everyone else. She turned around for one last look, in the process losing control of the moving chair, which rammed into a tree, causing Bridget to jerk forward.

A snake dropped from the tree into Bridget's lap.

Kate shrieked. The pale green snake, with a green and yellow head, was about a meter long. Its menacing eye-slits and flickering black tongue fixated on Bridget. Desperate to protect her, Kate instinctively lunged for it. The snake recoiled, and in a lightning-fast motion, bit Bridget on the hip. She barely stirred.

"No!" Kate yelled. She had to catch the snake in case it was venomous—she jumped forward and grabbed its tail. The snake attempted a strike, but she flung its body, slamming its head against the tree trunk. She then tossed it into the chair's side pocket.

Her trembling hands notwithstanding, she pulled desperately toward the tree line, grateful at the sight of Brothers and Sisters running toward her. The snake explained the rustling, but the other sound persisted. It was getting louder. She pushed away from the trees, but the soft soil, coupled with the grass, held up the chair. Her quaking hands slowed her attempt to dislodge the wheels from the muddy grooves. The sound grew louder. She yanked at the chair from the front. The chair yielded, but it was too late. A blaring sound like a ship horn heralded a large black mass emerging from the trees.

Kate stared in horror as the mass expanded, revealing thousands of wasps.

God, no!

She threw her body on top of Bridget. She heard a blood-curdling scream and then realized it was hers. Rolling over in agony, she felt sting after sting riddle her body.

"Bridget!" she called in despair as hundreds of the creatures descended and blanketed Bridget from head to toe. She tried to roll back onto Bridget to cover her, but the wasps covered her own face, causing her to double over in pain. Her eyes were swollen shut; she fell to the ground with a thud. She tried to breathe, but her breath was stuck in her swollen windpipe. Realizing that this breath was to be her final one, with her last bit of strength she grabbed a handful of earth.

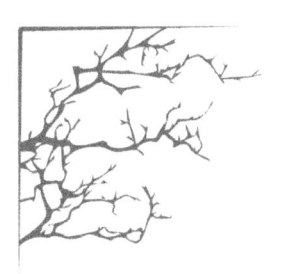

Chapter 20

"I CAN'T TAKE MY EYES off her, just knowing that she's still in there somewhere," Jeremy said. His wife looked increasingly pale. He kissed her forehead gently, grateful that he could make contact with her skin now that infections were no longer an issue of concern. She was already infected, and she was just hours away from dying.

Bridget's quick, ragged breaths pumped her chest cavity, in stark contrast to the eerie stillness of the rest of her body. Her skin sagged, distorting her features in the dim light of the infirmary.

"Do you think she's aware? Maybe just too weak to speak or touch?" Bede pulled up a chair next to the bed.

"She's always aware." Jeremy stood and paced around the room. "I have to burn up all this nervous energy. I can't believe the viral load. It's like anything and everything has descended into her bloodstream."

"Poor thing!" Bede held Bridget's hand.

The door to the infirmary opened with a squeak.

"Tasmi?" Bede walked up to the Colonel.

Tasmi put his arm around Bede and faced Jeremy. "Kate didn't make it. She passed away a few minutes ago."

"This is the worst day of my life," Jeremy said breathlessly.

Bede held his brother in a hug for a minute as they both wept for their departed friend.

"Was she Thysian?" Jeremy asked.

Bede nodded.

Jeremy inhaled and said softly, "Upon thy wings, O Lord."

"To thy breast, Sweet Mother," Bede and Tasmi replied in unison, tapping their fists on their chests.

"We'll make arrangements for the release of the body." Tasmi approached Bridget. "How is she?"

"We can't explain why she isn't dead yet. But it's coming." Jeremy spoke like a man emptied of all feeling. He took a deep breath and led Tasmi to a chair. All three men sat facing each other, next to Bridget's bed. They watched Bridget in silence for ten minutes.

"Tasmi," Jeremy broke the silence. "I called a friend of mine to borrow some lab equipment. She's about ten minutes away. Can you have it brought in uninspected? She can't get through the French soldiers."

"What are you up to?" asked Tasmi, ever curious.

"She's alive, but not for long. There's something I'd like to test while she's alive." He turned to Bede, whose brow furrowed in obvious curiosity.

"Sure. I'll be back shortly," Tasmi said as he hurried out of the room.

Bede eyed his brother. "I hope it's worth it. Tasmi will collect on this favor. He always does."

"It is."

"What do you have in mind?" Bede asked.

"I'm trying to think like she would." He gestured toward Bridget. "Why is she alive when she should be dead?"

Bede smiled sweetly at Bridget. "She would say... because she is living." He cocked his head slightly at his brother, raising his eyebrows. "You think she can survive this?"

"I just want to check."

"How?" Bede asked.

"If Tasmi can get the equipment, we can measure her cell generation rate while she's alive."

"Oh!" Bede stood up and stroked his chin. "Fractionate the blood without a centrifuge?"

"No. We don't want to separate out her blood. We just need to screen it for cell proliferation."

Both men huddled over a high desk by the bed and began sketching design ideas.

The door swung open an hour later as Tasmi's crisp steps filled the room, in contrast to the muted ones of the Brothers and Sisters, who came in and out periodically. He set two large aluminum cases on the floor. "She says that's the high-content imaging device, and the parts for what you're building are in the other one."

"Thank you," Bede said as he crouched to open the cases.

Tasmi squeezed Jeremy's shoulder as they both watched Bridget breathe. "She was a wonderful person. The world will miss what she could have been." He sighed. "Boys, I have to work to do. Jeremy, you know how to reach me. I want to know the moment anything changes with her."

"Thank you, Tasmi," Jeremy offered with a deep bow.

"Be well. Both of you." He responded with a bow.

Both men set to work, completing the contraption in two hours. They then attached a series of capillary tubes to various points in Bridget's body. The tubes led into a bulky pressurized container from which more tubes connected to Bridget's body. Next, they positioned and calibrated the imager and reprogrammed it to measure and report the results. They activated the device and watched as deep red blood flowed through the tubes, into the container, and back into Bridget.

Bridget's breathing remained shallow and weak. It would take at least thirty minutes before they would have any definitive results. Bede remained by Bridget's side while Jeremy walked around the room. There was no point in watching the numbers from second to second, or minute to minute. Jeremy had been awake four days now without much sleep. This time, though, he was energized. It was good to get his mind off everything and work with his brother on building something. Just like good old times.

When Bede's timer sounded thirty minutes later, they pored through the data.

"Could it be?" Jeremy's forehead knotted in confusion.

Bede studied Bridget's face carefully. "Both her red and white blood cell counts are up. The rate of mitosis is sustainable. She's not dying."

Jeremy beamed at Bede, mouth wide open. "She just might make it."

"Oh, my God, Bridget, you are a wonder," Bede said softly.

Jeremy ran to the door. "Get Sister Kaypore. Quickly, please," he said to the Sister seated outside the infirmary. He helped Bede remove the mini-IVs they'd used for their experiment.

Sister Kaypore hurried in, her gaze expectant.

Jeremy waved her over to the bedside. "She's not dying. Her body is regenerating."

Sister Kaypore scrutinized Bridget's face, laying a gentle hand on Bridget's chest. Her face twisted into a frown.

"What's wrong, Sister? You don't seem happy," Bede asked.

She reached into her pocket and pulled out an envelope. "This is a warrant from the DGSI, our domestic intelligence agency. It is for Bridget Blade's arrest. They are holding her responsible for all the deaths and injuries, both here on the grounds and beyond. They haven't taken her yet because she's dying, and they want to avoid an international incident."

"But she wasn't responsible." Bede wagged his finger at the Sister.

"In their eyes, she was," Sister Kaypore replied.

"Well, I'm sure we can clear all this up," Jeremy said.

"Don't you see?" Sister Kaypore shook her head. "It's an excuse."

"But, Sister," Bede said, "they wanted her corpse for scientific study. But she's alive now."

"Then she's of far more interest now, alive." She grabbed Jeremy's hand. "We have fellow Ryneans in the government who've been sending us information. The French Government will arrest her and say it's only for questioning, but in actuality, they will experiment on her under the guise of medical care. If and when she's healthy, they'll run a battery of psychological tests. She's a scientific miracle, a wonder, a curiosity. She's a treasure trove of the kind of information that can revolutionize science, war... if you let them take her... don't let them take her!"

"We have to get her out of here," Bede said.

Jeremy looked out of the window into the dark night. "I have an idea. It'll require some deception, and I am going to have to deal." Jeremy put on his jacket. "The U.S. government will want to do the same things the French want."

"Do whatever you need to do," Bede said. "I trust our government much more than I trust the French. We need to get her out of here before anyone has the same idea we had! Give Tasmi whatever he wants."

"Okay." Jeremy looked around to make sure he was not forgetting anything. "I'm going to Tasmi. I'll keep you posted."

Bede squeezed Bridget's hand as Jeremy closed the door behind him. "Hang in there, Sweetie. You keep fighting. We'll get you out of here."

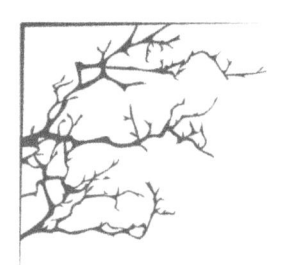

Chapter 21

JEREMY AND SISTER KAYPORE watched as Brothers Juan and Francois rolled a gurney with Kate's body on it into the lobby. Jeremy peered out of the main monastery entrance. The French guards, far beyond the pavilion, moved too much for him to predict their position, but he knew they were monitoring the monastery closely.

The dim lights made it hard to see the details of Kate's corpse. Jeremy wished for just a little more light. Kate looked like she was sleeping peacefully. Her face, puffy and pockmarked from the wasp stings, still retained its earnestness. All that was missing was that piercing gaze from those green eyes. Jeremy straightened her black dress and then laid a flower next to her. He let his hand linger on her waist, half hoping she would hold it, but she was gone. Kate had been judicious and discreet with all the information she'd garnered, and she had earned their trust. Finding people like her wasn't easy.

"I'll miss you," Jeremy whispered.

Brother Juan then wheeled the body into the elevator and went up to the second floor to a waiting Bede. Bede took a step to the side and looked at the corpse. He kissed her face and said a silent prayer.

Once in the infirmary, everyone set at different tasks but worked in unison. Ostensibly, Kate's corpse was brought in from the hospital so that the Order could perform a funeral rite, since she died on their grounds. As Jeremy hoped, the French security cordon did not see anything strange about that. Since they had inspected the casket coming in, it was unlikely they'd inspect it going out.

The Sisters removed Kate's body and placed it on a large, flower-strewn wooden pallet. The Sisters and Brothers set to work reconfiguring the casket with a false bottom for oxygen supply, medical equipment, and charcoal to scrub carbon dioxide. Others drilled holes for tubes. Finally, they moved Bridget and fitted her carefully into the modified casket.

Bede knelt by the casket. "Bridget, it's me, Bede. We're going to try to get you out of here. We're going to get you back home to the U.S. The ride may be bumpy, but hang in there, okay? We love you." He kissed her cheek.

Jeremy knelt on the other side. "Honey, I'll be with you every step of the way. I love you." He glanced up at Sister Kaypore and nodded. The Sisters screwed the hinges back on and covered up the casket. They all watched a monitor on the wall. All Bridget's vital signs remained as they had been earlier.

"The pressure in the casket is fine... and the oxygen level is good." Bede took a deep breath in relief.

Jeremy called out to the Brothers. "Can you bring Kate here? Let them say goodbye to each other one last time." Kate's corpse was laid next to Bridget. The living Bridget in the casket, and the dead Kate on the flower-strewn pallet. The room filled quickly with soft cries.

Sister Kaypore hugged Jeremy and held his face in her hands. "You must move quickly. The security group with our people in it has rotated to the front gate. You shouldn't have any trouble getting past the guards. From there, your friend takes over?"

"Yes. Tasmi has it all arranged. The U.S. military has a helicopter waiting to evacuate her to a base, and then she'll be transferred back stateside."

She enveloped Jeremy in a hug. "Thank you so much. I can never repay you for what you've done. But take care of my little girl." She kissed the confused Jeremy and turned to Bede. "You're the sweetest man I've ever known. For a priest of Thysia, you're not half-bad." Everyone laughed. She kissed him on both cheeks.

"I speak for Bridget when I say that we are forever in your debt. I promise to repay your kindness. Ryna has been unfairly blamed for all that happened here. I promise you, I will do everything in my power to restore Ryna to her greatness, and to restore her honor." Jeremy struggled to keep a hushed, steady tone, but he could not hide his overwhelming gratitude. His fingers touched his lips and blew a gentle kiss.

Heavy steps sounded down the corridor, and a Brother rushed in. He whispered in Sister Kaypore's ears.

Her eyes widened. "Did you tell them we're performing the funeral rite?"

The Brother nodded. "They insist on being here and will present the warrant afterward. They were waiting on the elevator, but Sister Mark is holding it on the fifth floor. We have very little time."

"Sister?" a Brother asked. "What's wrong?"

"The police are here," she said.

One of the Sisters peered out the window. "They've surrounded the building."

"I thought the agreement was fifty meters out." Bede looked out the window.

"I should never have let the Marines go." Jeremy bit his lip. He lifted his phone to his ear and pulled it back. "They're jamming the signal."

"Sister Lacey, Brother Micah, Jeremy, Bede, bring Bridget now and follow me," she said, closing Bridget's casket. She turned to the rest. "You all know what to do. Do not make it easy, give no ground." She curled her finger at one of the sisters who ran toward her. "Bring the ropes, bolts, and harnesses down to me in the cavern room."

Sister Kaypore rushed out of the infirmary with Jeremy, Bede, and the others struggling to keep up as they carried the casket. "Hurry!" she said, holding the door to the staircase open. "All the way down to the cavern room."

The quartet moved quickly down the stairs with Bridget as quietly as they could manage, careful to avoid hitting the rails. Finally, at the bottom, Sister Kaypore locked the stairwell door behind them. A few moments later, the beeps of a keypad and the welcome sound of sliding doors filled the corridor. The cavern hall sat bare and empty.

"Micah, wait by the stairs and open the door *only* if it is Sister Payne with the climbing equipment." She turned to the other Sister. "Remain by the elevator and keep anyone who comes occupied for as long as you can."

"Are we going to take Bridget through the cavern shaft?" Bede asked, his forehead knotted in worry.

"It's our only hope of getting her out of here," she said, locking the doors behind them. "We train to climb through the shaft. We can do it."

"Bede, help me," Jeremy said, picking up one end of the casket. "Let's get her to the glass wall."

They waited for a few minutes, with Sister Kaypore frequently craning her neck at the doors to see down the corridor.

"They must have fanned out and prevented Sister Payne from bringing down the equipment." Sister Kaypore pounded a fist against her palm.

"I have friends I can call," Jeremy said to the pacing sister.

"I'll need you to do that," she responded. "I don't want them taking any blood from her." She walked up to the casket and stared at Bridget, who seemed oblivious to all the activity.

A loud crash, followed by loud voices, interrupted them. "They're here."

"Sister Kaypore, we have a warrant for Bridget Blade. Please open this door!" The voice, faint through the double doors, was still audible from the far end of the hall.

"They'll break the door," Jeremy said. "Let me talk to them."

"No, Jeremy," Sister Kaypore said. "I must do something here." She knelt by the casket and tapped Bridget's shoulder repeatedly. "Bridget! Bridget! Theresa Bridget, answer me!"

Jeremy and Bede knelt across from her. "What are you doing?" Jeremy asked, reaching his hand out to stop her.

"Theresa Bridget, if you can hear me, you have to help me!"

"Sister! What is going on?" Jeremy spoke sharply.

Bridget stirred and moaned softly. Her eyes fluttered and then became still.

Sister Kaypore traced her hands around Bridget's cheekbones and down to her chin. "You were always such a sweet baby. I love you with all my heart. I know I couldn't be there with you all these years, but you've come to me now. In your world, there are no coincidences. Things are what they are supposed to be. I know one thing that must be. The Selites must live unsullied. If you are captured, they will be, too, and eternity will be infected by the stain of evil. Please, my dear, release them to hide. They can return later, but for now, we're trapped. There's nowhere to go."

"Sister?" Bede asked.

She raised her index finger to her lips and stood slowly. She backed up slowly, motioning the men to follow her. She held both men firmly by the wrist. "Swear to me that what you see here today, you will never reveal to anyone, nor will you ever speak of it."

"Sister," Bede said. "What—"

"Swear it, by Lord Rynae na Haru!"

"May it be done to me and more, if I break this oath." Both men recited the oath.

Bridget moaned again. She then whispered, but too low for the three of them to hear her words. The sounds of the banging at the door and the calls of the police faded as a crackling sound rose from the box.

Sister Kaypore gripped both men by the wrist. "Do not say a word of whatever you see. Think good thoughts. Let's think about Bridget, her love, her smile, anything that makes you happy. But from now until this is over, we stay silent."

The crackling sound continued until a thick black fluid filled the casket. The bubbling fluid glinted and sparkled, even in the low light of the hall. Slowly the fluid swelled like a cresting wave and, at its high point, it began to solidify until a large human-shaped figure stood before them. Another one emerged, and another, until five of them stood by Bridget's casket.

Sister Kaypore, suppressing a gasp of her own, kept her grip tight on the men. All five Selites, tall and thin, like fragile crystals, swayed gently. They gathered around Bridget and crouched. She couldn't see what they were doing. Their arms appeared busy, and then each one kissed Bridget. All five stood and faced the three humans. One of the Selites pointed at Sister Kaypore and smiled. She let go of the men and gave a slight wave. She walked slowly to the door of the cavern, unlocked it and opened it wide.

The Selites took careful, measured steps toward the door and out onto the landing where, days ago, Bridget had triggered this entire episode, and where, weeks ago, a sweet young sister had performed the Euthanasia. Holding each other, the Selites morphed into a black fluid, spreading out over the base of the landing. The thick black fluid flowed toward the rock face and seeped into it until there was no longer any trace of them.

The thumping continued outside.

"What—or—who were those?" Jeremy asked, unable to stop his heart from racing.

Sister Kaypore looked at both men sternly. "You swore an oath to me before the Lord. Not a word of this must ever be spoken again, not to me, not to each other." She paused as both men nodded. "I think the police have indulged me enough. If I don't answer the door, they will knock it down."

"We can't let them take her," Bede said.

"I still have clout here," Sister Kaypore said. "Let me handle this."

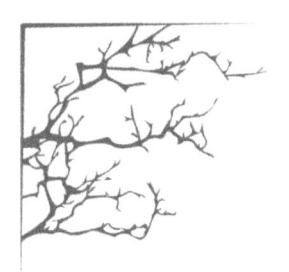

Chapter 22

SISTER KAYPORE OPENED the first set of double glass doors and stood at the next set of doors. Just beyond, a crowd of policemen stood waiting. She craned her neck to see who else was there. *Brother Micah. Colonel Singh.* She breathed a sigh of relief. If Singh was here, then his Marine was close by.

She unlocked the door and waited. No one moved—not toward her, not away from her. They all watched, as though waiting for her instruction.

"Brother Micah, Sister Lacey, help Jeremy and Padre Bede. Take Bridget to the lobby." Sister Kaypore felt relief as her voice carried as strongly as she'd hoped. "Colonel Singh, would you please escort them?"

A path formed in the midst of her pursuers as Brother Micah, Sister Lacey, and Tasmi rushed into the cavern room, followed by a tall Marine, who backed in slowly.

"Sister, would you come with us... please?" One of the police asked. He was a tall man, with a long face and a thick mustache.

Sister Kaypore hesitated, looking back toward the sounds in the cavern hall.

"We promise," he said, "they will be allowed to take Dr. Blade to the lobby uninterrupted."

Sister Kaypore nodded and followed the man. They hurried down the hallway and got into the elevator. "I will go up with Sister, alone." The man extended his arm to prevent anyone else from getting in the elevator. Once the door closed, he turned to her. "Sister, if you can get

THE CLAY QUEEN

the woman to the south side of the monastery, we have people in the woods who can take her to safety."

Sister Kaypore's shoulders dropped in relief. He was a fellow Rynean. "What's the situation out there?"

"The lobby is full of people, and our forces are all through the monastery. On the grounds, there are additional police, but not many."

She held his hand and squeezed gratefully. "Tell your people to be ready. I can get her out of here." She unlocked the elevator door and both waited until it arrived at the lobby. She gasped at the sheer number of people waiting. Not bothering to speak to anyone, she rushed to her right and ran for the kitchen.

"Sister!" Brother Juan's voice called to her.

Sister Kaypore turned and motioned him into the large kitchen. Other sisters and brothers ran toward them.

"Run out to the potato patch and harvest as many green potatoes and new potato sprouts as you can." She said to the left side of the group that had gathered. Turning to the group of her sisters on her right, she said. "Make drinks, tea, coffee, juices... jello."

"Sister, what are we doing?" Brother Juan asked.

She took a deep breath. "We have an opportunity to get Bridget out of here, but we must get her past all those people in the lobby and into the woods."

Brother Juan clapped his hands and spoke loudly. "Be discreet. Time is of the essence." The group of brothers and sisters scattered to their tasks. He turned back to Sister Kaypore. "You wish to poison our guests?"

She nodded.

"Potato poisoning will take hours to work."

"I know," she said, "but it's all I can think of right now."

"It is a drastic option, Sister. We will do it if you ask it of us, even—"

"Juan." She hugged him tightly. "I don't want to drag you, or anyone else, into this. I am proposing to take lives that Lord Ryna has not sanctioned to be taken."

"Kay, you are not from this world."

Sister Kaypore gasped.

"We all know that," he said. "I don't know who you are or what you've seen. I don't know where you're from or why you're here. I even know that, secretly, you love Thysia and bear no ill will toward her. You are special, and so dear to us. Our faith eschews leaders, but we are all sworn to follow you wherever you lead. You bear a burden no one should bear alone. We'll bear that weight with you."

"What other options do I have, Juan?"

"Let's harness our worldwide numbers and the devotion of our people. Give me time to see what I can arrange."

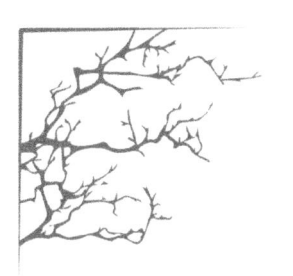

Chapter 23

SISTER KAYPORE PRESSED her hands against her closed eyes in an effort to relieve the pressure building in her head. The scene was surreal. Bridget lay unconscious in a casket balanced precariously on a gurney. The lobby swarmed with people—the French, U.S. government officials, including the Ambassador; Vatican personnel; and two people from the Chinese embassy.

Jeremy had been on the phone intermittently for the thirty minutes since they were forced back up here from the cavern room. Bede, a few feet from Jeremy, was engaged in an animated conversation with a representative from the Vatican. It wasn't clear what progress he'd made, if any, but he certainly wasn't letting her leave without obtaining a favorable commitment. Colonel Tasmi Singh moved from person to person. He seemed to know everyone, and he appeared to have the respect of everyone. He'd spent time talking to the intelligence representatives, the French military, the police, and the Chinese ambassador.

Jeremy hovered protectively over Bridget. He adjusted her oxygen mask and smoothed her hair. A sister checked her blood pressure and whispered in Jeremy's ear. At the foot of the casket, the Marine stood at the ready in his combat fatigues. He seemed immobile, but his eyes scanned the lobby and his right arm was bent slightly at the elbow, positioning his fingers lightly on his unlatched holster. If Jeremy's glares were not enough to keep the French medics away, the Marine's presence did the trick.

Three feet away, and no closer, two men periodically argued with Jeremy. They insisted that Bridget exhibited signs of a brain injury and needed urgent medical care, pointing to a mobile CT scan unit stationed at the entrance to the lobby. Regardless of the intensity of their pleas, Jeremy remained unmoved. Earlier, for a fleeting moment, Sister Kaypre had wondered if perhaps Bridget won't be better served with proper medical care, even if it meant submitting her to French custody and inevitable experimentation. If Sister Kaypore had had a speck of doubt about the wisdom of their actions, Jeremy devotion to Bridget had removed them.

Sister Lacey came up to Sister Kaypore and whispered, "Would you like us to serve our guests? We're ready."

Sister Kaypore looked around at the sisters and brothers who'd filtered in and waited at the edges of the lobby. They stood next to rolling food trays filled with jugs of water, iced tea, and juices, all poisoned. It would be an act of ultimate desperation, perhaps an overreaction in her moment of doubt. She smiled at the young sister and shook her head. "Take them back. We will do this another way." She inhaled in relief as her brothers and sisters melted away.

She had to do something. Too much of her hope had been placed in others. She had a card to play and it was time.

She sighed as she waited for Monsieur Pierre to get off the phone. He was in charge of domestic law enforcement, and he was an easy one to read—patently ambitious and unwilling to take risks.

"Sister, I'm sorry," he said. "We must proceed with taking Bridget Blade into custody."

"She's in no condition," said Sister Kaypore. "Can't you at least wait until she improves?"

"We would be happy to provide for her medical care. I'm sure we can do better than you have."

"You take my threat lightly, don't you?"

Monsieur Pierre chuckled. "That all Ryneans the world over will descend on France and demand that she be released? With all due respect, Sister, this is not a real threat."

Sister Kaypore motioned to Brother Juan, who was leaning against the wall, and gave a barely perceptible nod.

"Wait!" Monsieur Pierre said. "You can't be serious? Your God is already so scandalized for her cruel murder of thousands. Would you risk the potential scorn that would rain down on her if millions of your people descended on France?"

Sister Kaypore raised her hand discreetly in Brother Juan's direction. "Ten million Ryneans in the next seven days. They will come in by plane, by boat, by train—legally, illegally—and it'll be blamed on you. I need a yes or a no, Monsieur."

"You bluff, Madame," he hissed. "Thousands dead. Thousands injured—"

"Ryna gives and she takes. She has reaped those souls for her glory. It is what we live for." She stepped closer to him. "She's taken thousands of lives, and thousands more will slip into her bosom in the next few days. What is one more to her? Would you threaten me? Bridget? And risk confronting my God?"

His nose flared. "I don't fear you or your blood-thirsty God. She is an imposter."

"You should," Sister Kaypore replied. "We all do. And if I call, millions will answer because of the fear of Ryna. We live for one thing and one thing alone: Euthanasia, the beautiful death. We are willing martyrs. We will gladly die at our own hand for Ryna—at the borders, at the seaports, at the airports. Will such deaths heap more scorn on Ryna? Possibly. But imagine what it would do to the image of France, with pictures of thousands of dead Ryneans published all around the world, all because you won't let us care for this one woman."

"Who is she? She's nobody. She just—"

"She is everything to me, to the Order, and to all Ryneans." She inhaled and laid a hand on his arm. "I don't want to fight. Let her be, Monsieur. Just for tonight. Let her rest and recover. Tomorrow, you can all discuss what is to be done with her."

"Damn you and your disgusting, blood-drinking religion." He glared at her. "I'll talk to the President's people. We'll see what they say. For tonight, she may remain here." He wagged his finger in her face. "Your American friends can no longer protect you. Tomorrow, I send men in here and we take that woman. We are well within our rights." He stormed past her, bumping her rudely and knocking her to the floor.

She watched as he walked away in a huff.

"Are you okay, Sister?" Brother Juan reached out and helped her up.

She held both his hands. "I am responsible for Bridget Blade. Send word out. By morning, I want thousands of our people on planes, on boats, in cars; I want them to flood the borders. It's the only way the government will back down. Otherwise, we lose her and, once she's gone, we may never get her back."

"Yes, Sister." Brother Juan bowed and hurried away.

Head down, she weaved through the people until she reached Jeremy, who was now huddled with Tasmi and Bede.

"I've got the Chinese pretty worked up about all this," Tasmi said. "As much as Bridget is our citizen, she's also theirs, and I spooked him with talk of how each citizen is a battleground and to yield at this point is an erosion of sovereignty. Their government is going to insist that any procedure done on Bridget without the full consent of the Chinese government will have grave repercussions on relations."

"I can't get anywhere," Jeremy said, eyes reddened and brows furrowed. "I've called the President and some Senators, and no one wants to touch this. Ryna is toxic right now—not one to be associated with. What good is access if it gains you nothing? All that power and influence I thought I had was just an illusion."

"It's not over, Jeremy," Sister Kaypore said. "I've gotten concessions from the French. They'll let us keep her here tonight, and then we can bargain for more in the days to come. Tasmi's got the Chinese involved—"

"And the Vatican will scale back its support for the French," Bede said. "They don't want to be associated with human experimentation, which I emphasized was what the French want."

"How is she?" Sister Kaypore asked, leaning over the casket.

"She's barely stirred, even with all this noise and movement," Jeremy said.

"Let's take her upstairs," Sister Kaypore said. "At least she'll be safe for tonight."

Jeremy, Bede, Sister Kaypore, and Tasmi gathered around Bridget after they'd settled her back in the infirmary.

"It's heartbreaking to see her this way," Bede said. "She was always so full of life. If and when she regains consciousness, she'll have to live with that unbearable pain until we can find a way to release it from her. It'll change her. But I'll take a changed Bridget over no Bridget any day."

Jeremy patted his brother on the back, turned, and walked toward the infirmary door.

"Where are you going?" Tasmi asked.

Jeremy turned to the group and exhaled loudly. "Every single night, I have to coax Bridget to sleep because she's frightened to death that the world will still be the same when she wakes. Every morning, she wakes up horrified and disoriented and sometimes it takes hours to stabilize her. Every time she is not in my presence, I am worried about her, about what she's doing. The last time I got anything close to a full night's uninterrupted sleep was last year when she lay dying from eating wild mushrooms. She's the focal point of international tension. No one is going to touch her tonight. And she is surrounded by people who love her and who will sustain her."

He took a step backward toward the door. "It is a rare confluence of events. Bridget is sedated and barely conscious. She may actually, for once, be at rest, free of anxiety, unaware of her own pain. Bede, the only person who cares for Bridget as much as I do, is here. Sister Kaypore, you've only just met Bridget, or at least, so I thought. But you know something about her that the rest of us don't. And I know you love her deeply. Tasmi, you've never cared about anyone in your life, but Bridget counts you as a special friend—that has to count for something." Jeremy winked, causing Tasmi to chuckle. "Every single brother and sister of the Order seems to overflow with love and devotion. For once, I do not have to be Bridget's anchor. It is most certainly the rarest of coincidences, and I will take advantage of it. Tomorrow, we fight again for her as we've always done, but tonight, I sleep."

SISTER KAYPORE WOKE with a start at the squeaking sound coming from the main infirmary room. She gripped the chair's armrests as she oriented herself, remembering that she was in the side infirmary room.

Bridget!

She waited for her eyes to adjust to the darkness and stood slowly, not wanting to alert whoever was making the noise. It was unlikely that anyone would attempt anything with Bridget tonight, but the Order members were all strategically positioned to keep an eye on all the different interests whose representatives were still present. She was supposed to be watching Bridget, but had fallen asleep.

The main infirmary room was dimly lit, and a tall, dark figure was hunched over her bed—it was Jeremy. She could tell from his tall, athletic frame, and his profile.

It's 3 a.m.? What is he doing?

The medical monitors were all black. He must have unplugged them. She could see the silhouette of his arms as he worked around Bridget's body. Stepping back, he held three IV lines and twisted them around the bed rail. From the base of the bed, he opened a nightgown, sky blue with a lace panel top, and worked to get it on her. His strong, confident arms moved gently as he dressed Bridget.

Bridget's hair. It's grown! Not possible!

Jeremy positioned his wife on her side and began to work her hair into long, loose braids. A few minutes later, he did the same on the other side. His torso blocked Sister Kaypore's view and she couldn't tell what he was doing, except that he leaned over Bridget's face. As he straightened, he placed a makeup brush on the dresser next to the bed.

He stood back and assessed his handiwork. Then he lifted Bridget off the bed. His steps sounded crisply in the silence of the monastery as he carried her to the other end of the room and sat down gently on one of the large, comfortable leather chairs that had been set up in the room. Bridget, wrapped in his arms, oblivious to the world, remained unconscious.

Sister Kaypore remained still, savoring this rare peek into the sanctuary of this relationship. She'd spoken with Jeremy for the first time on the phone only a few days ago, although she'd known of him for years as she monitored Bridget's progress. He was a highly-esteemed theoretician, but she'd never quite known what to make of him, or whether he was right for Bridget. However, in the few hours she'd spent with Bridget's people, she'd come to understand their absolute trust in providence. If Jeremy was Bridget's husband, then he was meant to be her husband. In the past few days, Sister Kaypore had warmed to him and come to appreciate him. If there was anyone who could have more concern for Bridget than she did, it was Jeremy. And that gave her comfort beyond measure.

Sister Kaypore couldn't tell if Jeremy had fallen asleep. He was motionless, and his breathing was rhythmic and steady. She slipped through the curtain and slid down the wall until she was on the floor with a good view of him. He had sunk into the chair, his head rested against Bridget's, and his arms cradled her torso. Her legs hung over his thighs, revealing her calves and bare feet in the soft light of the infirmary. This was the power of Bridget, the eros she inspired, causing the mighty to desire nothing but her and her will.

Now Sister Kaypore understood the truth that had eluded her for so many years. Her understanding of Bridget had been clouded by her doubts and her inability to see beyond the weak, fragile baby she'd brought to this world many years ago. Jeremy, on the other hand, never doubted. He believed in everything that she could be and more, and now Sister Kaypore saw what she'd never before been able to see—Bridget, fragile and vulnerable, but every bit the queen, every bit a god. And Jeremy, her throne.

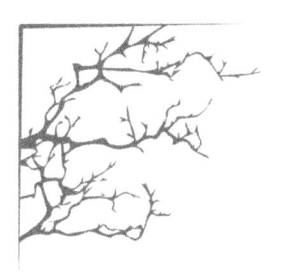

Epilogue

SO SHE SLEEPS.

And so *I* sleep.

Her frailty echoes to me over the channel of time. I ache to comfort her, to love her, to assure her that she can survive and live to be me. I wish nothing more than to strengthen her in the belief that a mortal may achieve immortality, and that a woman born of man may indeed become *me*, Queen Nouei, God of this earth—that she may live the paradox of being born from the very seeds she nurtured in eternity.

I cannot walk her path, nor can I guide her way. She must become, of her own power, what she is to be. All I can do is call out to her. All that I can share with her is that the birth of a god must begin with love. She must learn love, pure love, and only then will she grow to be divine.

But what is love?

Love begins with a promise. It *is* a promise. It is a script whose truth is revealed only when it is complete. The truth of love is discerned from the perspective of the future, when all our lovers' deeds are finished and open for scrutiny and judgment. When we look back and examine our lovers' actions in all cases, then, and only then, may we indeed know if their love was true.

I have known love from two people. You will meet my greatest love, my ally in my struggle against Lord Ryna. But if she is to be my greatest love, then she must be a god, because, in truth, only a god can love a god truly. Like Bridget, I must nurture her and set her on the road to divinity. Her love is, and ever will be, an unending promise.

When my story is done, I will have walked through the entire curtain of all possibilities, of all possible worlds. I have searched for that special man who could love me, and genuinely so, whose love for me does not depend on the bounty I bestow, whose worship is not anchored to my beneficence. Do I dare hope that among men I might find one to promise such love to me?

I have known of no such man who holds firm in his devotion even when we gods withhold our blessing, except one. This is the one enslaved to me, who holds me as a throne, a man I will encounter over and over and over again, who, without fail, would sacrifice all for me, whose life is of no account to himself and who would die for me without hesitation. His love is a true promise, which is all I ask of those who follow me.

But as much as Bridget must learn that love is a promise, she must understand that love is a vow.

It is no task to love Lord Ryna, for she is beauty itself; She is that which cannot but be desired. It is no task for me to love myself, for I am the eternal womb, that in which the bounty of Ryna is revealed. The love of God, the vow of God, must be steadfast both in the face of the eternal and in the presence of the frail.

Bridget's vow will prove true and eternal. It must, if she is to persist until my present time. Bridget... I... have vowed to love a man, a feeble mound of clay animated by the breath I give it. You may mock me and sneer at my choices. For does not a vow, once given, bind eternally? And does not a bond with the weaker hollow out the strong? Have we not then foolishly bound ourselves to that which is unworthy of our glory?

I assure you that neither I, nor Bridget, are the victims you may think.

I am as ruthless as I am loving. And I will vindicate my vow as I will the devotion of that man who has loved me. I will imbue him with a fierce jealousy for me. He will be my sword, to crush without mercy all those who have mocked me. I will be ruthless to the Jaru, and the Fenti, and those of the Low Country who have abandoned me. Zeal for me

THE CLAY QUEEN 141

shall consume this man, and he will execute my ruthlessness throughout the earth until I regain supremacy... *if* I regain my supremacy.

Love is also mercy.

When my enemies arrive at my gates in a fortnight, if I have failed in my plan, I know in my heart that I would desire their mercy. I do not wish to be humiliated in the presence of the very people who worship me, nor do I wish this magnificent temple to fall into disrepair.

If I fail, I will entreat Ryna and implore her mercy. I will implore her to command her people to treat me with kindness.

I am a god, but I am not perfect in love yet. I am the primordial clay, still on the potter's wheel until I become what even Ryna will be proud of—her daughter. I understand love as a promise or vow. Maybe, in four thousand years, I... Bridget... will learn love as mercy. Maybe then we will be the perfect god.

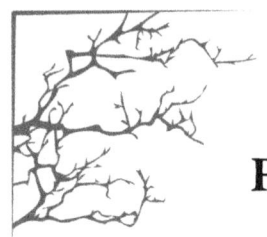

From the Author

THANK YOU FOR READING *The Clay Queen*. If you enjoyed this book, please show your support with a review on Amazon or Goodreads.

For updates on upcoming novels or more about this world I am creating, visit my website: www.onoekeh.com.

THE CHILDREN OF CLAY series
  Series Prequel: She Died in My Arms[1]
  Book 1: The Clay Queen
  Book 2: Clay to Ashes[2]
  Book 3: Icon of Clay[3]

---

1. https://www.amazon.com/dp/B07BC4WTWR
2. https://www.amazon.com/dp/B075JK2QPN
3. https://www.amazon.com/dp/B0774NQ2QJ